HOTSHOT IN HIGH GEAR!

Frank kicked down one gear, dangerously over-revving his engine but gaining a burst of acceleration that finally brought him alongside the stranger. He couldn't make out the newcomer's face behind the tinted visor, but he waved for his rival to stop.

The other rider ignored Frank's warning, gunning the engine of the fancy European bike and racing forward. Directly ahead was Devil's Gap! Frank and Joe both veered off the trail, hoping their companion would do the same.

No—the other bike just rocketed on. All the Hardys could do was watch in horror as the rider roared full speed toward the edge!

Books in THE HARDY BOYS CASEFILES™ Series

#1 DEAD ON TARGET
#2 EVIL, INC.
#3 CULT OF CRIME
#4 THE LAZARUS PLOT
#5 EDGE OF DESTRUCTION
#6 THE CROWNING TERROR
#7 DEATHGAME
#8 SEE NO EVIL
#9 THE GENIUS THIEVES
#12 PERFECT GETAWAY
#13 THE BORGIA DAGGER
#14 TOO MANY TRAITORS
#24 SCENE OF THE CRIME
#29 THICK AS THIEVES
#30 THE DEADLIEST DARE
#32 BLOOD MONEY
#33 COLLISION COURSE
#35 THE DEAD SEASON
#37 DANGER ZONE
#41 HIGHWAY ROBBERY
#42 THE LAST LAUGH
#44 CASTLE FEAR
#45 IN SELF-DEFENSE
#46 FOUL PLAY
#47 FLIGHT INTO DANGER
#48 ROCK 'N' REVENGE
#49 DIRTY DEEDS
#50 POWER PLAY
#52 UNCIVIL WAR
#53 WEB OF HORROR
#54 DEEP TROUBLE
#55 BEYOND THE LAW
#56 HEIGHT OF DANGER
#57 TERROR ON TRACK
#58 SPIKED!
#60 DEADFALL
#61 GRAVE DANGER
#62 FINAL GAMBIT
#63 COLD SWEAT
#64 ENDANGERED SPECIES
#65 NO MERCY
#66 THE PHOENIX EQUATION
#67 LETHAL CARGO
#68 ROUGH RIDING
#69 MAYHEM IN MOTION
#70 RIGGED FOR REVENGE
#71 REAL HORROR
#72 SCREAMERS
#73 BAD RAP
#74 ROAD PIRATES
#75 NO WAY OUT
#76 TAGGED FOR TERROR
#77 SURVIVAL RUN
#78 THE PACIFIC CONSPIRACY
#79 DANGER UNLIMITED
#80 DEAD OF NIGHT
#81 SHEER TERROR
#82 POISONED PARADISE
#83 TOXIC REVENGE
#84 FALSE ALARM
#85 WINNER TAKE ALL
#86 VIRTUAL VILLAINY
#87 DEAD MAN IN DEADWOOD
#88 INFERNO OF FEAR
#89 DARKNESS FALLS
#90 DEADLY ENGAGEMENT
#91 HOT WHEELS
#92 SABOTAGE AT SEA
#93 MISSION: MAYHEM
#94 A TASTE FOR TERROR
#95 ILLEGAL PROCEDURE
#96 AGAINST ALL ODDS
#97 PURE EVIL
#98 MURDER BY MAGIC
#99 FRAME-UP
#100 TRUE THRILLER
#101 PEAK OF DANGER
#102 WRONG SIDE OF THE LAW
#103 CAMPAIGN OF CRIME
#104 WILD WHEELS

WILD WHEELS

FRANKLIN W. DIXON

AN ARCHWAY PAPERBACK
Published by POCKET BOOKS
New York London Toronto Sydney Tokyo Singapore

This book is a work of fiction. Names, characters, places and incidents are products of the author's imagination or are used fictitiously. Any resemblance to actual events or locales or persons, living or dead, is entirely coincidental.

AN ARCHWAY PAPERBACK *Original*

An Archway Paperback published by
POCKET BOOKS, a division of Simon & Schuster Inc.
1230 Avenue of the Americas, New York, NY 10020

Produced by Mega-Books, Inc.

ISBN: 0-671-88215-5

First Archway Paperback printing October 1995

10 9 8 7 6 5 4 3 2 1

Cover art by Brian Kotzky

Printed in the U.S.A.

IL 6+

WILD WHEELS

Chapter 1

"I'M BORED!" Joe Hardy declared to no one in particular. He glanced around the cafeteria, then back at his friends Tony Prito and Biff Hooper, and his older brother, Frank.

Joe hunkered forward, shifting his muscular frame around in the small chair. He ran a strong hand through his blond hair and narrowed his blue eyes for emphasis. "Don't take it personally, guys," he said. "It's not you. It's just that the school routine is starting to get to me. We haven't had any action in weeks—not since school started."

"Life's rough," Frank Hardy said sarcastically. "We've gone almost a month without discovering a single corpse or being shot at. I can understand how you'd miss that, Joe."

Biff and Tony chuckled. Joe gazed across the table at his lean, dark-haired brother. "You're right," Joe admitted. "There are plenty of other ways to have fun."

"It's been a long time since we rolled out our dirt bikes," Frank added.

Joe perked up instantly. "Great idea, Frank," he said. "We could blast around in Hopkins Woods like we used to." He turned to Biff and Tony. "What do you say, guys?"

"Sounds great," Tony answered. "But I've got gymnastics after school."

"And I promised my mom I'd rake," Biff added. "I've been putting it off for days, and I'm running out of excuses." Joe could see from Biff's wistful expression that he would rather rev up a dirtbike than rake leaves.

"Excuse me," a girl's voice piped up. "Are you guys talking about motorcycles?"

The four boys turned toward a very pretty girl sitting alone at the next table. She had auburn hair cut short, and her eyes were a striking green. The length of her legs was accentuated by tight jeans and a pair of red cowboy boots. She was wearing a black T-shirt—a black leather jacket was draped over the back of the chair beside her.

"Uh, yeah," said Biff, who was always a bit

tongue-tied around a pretty girl. *"They* are, any-way," he added, indicating Joe and Frank.

"Where are you going to ride?" she asked, turning her full attention to Frank.

Frank described the dirt bike trails around Hopkins Woods. "Why the interest?" he asked. "Would you like to come watch?"

"I just might," she said with a slight smile. "I like bikes." She stood up and slung her leather jacket over her shoulder. "See you around," she said to Frank, and walked off. The attention of all four boys was focused on her until she left the cafeteria.

"Wow, who's that?" Joe asked.

"She's new," Frank told him. "Her name's Lindsey Nichols. She's in my math class. Cute, huh?"

"Cute doesn't begin to do her justice," Joe answered. "She's gorgeous! And she sure seems to like you."

"Nah, she was just flirting. It doesn't mean anything."

"What doesn't mean anything?" asked Callie Shaw, Frank's steady girlfriend, as she plunked her lunch tray down next to Frank's. Callie had blond hair and soft brown eyes.

"Frank has a new admirer," Tony teased. Frank shot his friend a withering glance. Callie noticed the exchange.

"You must mean Lindsey," Callie said brightly.

"I saw you talking to her while I was getting my lunch. She could use more friends—it's hard being the new kid, especially in senior year. So long as it's just friends, right, pal?" she asked, leaning against Frank and playfully poking him in the ribs with her elbow.

"Absolutely," he said.

"Can you give me a hand with this, Joe?" Frank called to his brother as he struggled to ease a battered dirt bike out of the back of their black van. Joe's bike already stood parked on its sidestand in the open field adjacent to Hopkins Woods. Joe was tweaking the throttle, his head cocked to listen to the engine note of the small but powerful single-cylinder two-stroke engine. Frank had to shout over the racket to get Joe's attention.

"Oh, sure—sorry!" Joe quickly turned away from his machine and hustled over to help Frank. Together they lifted Frank's bike out of the van and set it down on the ground. Joe admired his brother's bike, even though it was almost identical to his own. They were both the same make, model, and year: three-year-old Trailbuster 250s—tall, lightweight, knobby-tired, spindly machines without lights or speedometers. Frank's was red—Joe's blue.

Dirt bikes were designed to do one thing well—blast through terrain that nothing else could tackle. The boys' bikes were battered, with chipped paint and dents and dings, but mechanically they were perfect. Their suspensions were taut, the transmissions shifted smoothly every time, and the brakes gripped powerfully.

Frank and Joe knew that the margin between having an accident and not was narrow. Equipment that wasn't superbly maintained could spell disaster. They no longer rode these bikes as much as they had in their early teens, but they still kept them up for just such an occasion as that beautiful early autumn afternoon. Now their attention to detail was about to be rewarded.

Frank made certain his gas tank was full. He checked his bike over once more, then stomped down on the kick starter. The engine fired to life with a roar. He pulled on his helmet and gloves as he glanced down at his clean riding leathers. He and Joe both wore custom white leather off-road suits, with stripes across the chest and down the arms, complete with shoulder pads, spine protectors, and full body armor. He smiled to himself. Their leathers wouldn't stay clean for long. He grinned over at Joe.

Joe flipped his older brother a thumbs-up sign. "You don't really think you can keep up with me, do you?" he shouted over the racket of the engines.

"You can't beat me on your best day and my worst!" Frank yelled back.

"Prove it!" Joe shouted, yanking back on the throttle of his bike. He shot forward into the woods. Frank cranked back hard on the right handgrip of his own bike. His front wheel kicked up into a wheelie, and he raced into the woods a split second behind Joe.

The Hardys had learned to ride on these trails. They had started riding young when their father, detective Fenton Hardy, bought them tiny trail bikes, and took them out on weekends. By the time they were teenagers they knew every inch of the woods, every trail. But furrows and gullies shift with the seasons, and no matter how well they knew Hopkins Woods, the trails would always present fresh challenges.

They bounced onto the dirt bike course the park service maintained. With the place seemingly all to themselves they could cut loose. They zoomed around fallen trees, massive boulders, and other obstacles, wrestling with the handlebars to keep their machines upright. First one took the lead, then the other. They constantly challenged each other.

Joe led Frank in a high-speed chase through a wild mass of underbrush. As they came out of the thicket a wide straightaway opened before them, a clear dirt trail barely two bikes wide, running along the top of a ridge for more than half a mile. Now they cranked their throttles full open, trying to squeeze every last bit of speed out of their engines as they raced along the ridge.

Halfway down the ridge, they were startled to hear the roar of another engine racing up behind them. Before they could react another bike hurtled by, cutting between them with an impossibly narrow margin of safety. The new rider sped ahead, then pulled up to an abrupt halt, spinning around to face the Hardys as they slowed. Just as quickly the rider taunted Frank and Joe with an exaggerated one-handed salute and took off back into the woods. The Hardys revved up and chased after the rider.

Frank was in awe of the rider's skills, and he knew Joe must also be amazed. The rider was on a big, new, expensive European machine. Ability counted for a lot, though, and usually Frank and Joe could match any rider on the slickest equipment. But not that day. The newcomer purposely led them on a wild chase. Whoever it was was a great rider, and the challenge of keeping up was making their afternoon.

The fun almost ended when Joe skidded sideways through a patch of mud. He put one foot down to steady himself, but the wheels of his bike kicked out, and he fell heavily, splashing mud up all around him as his bike landed on its side.

Frank slid to a stop beside his brother as Joe was climbing out of the mud. "You okay?" Frank asked. "Any injuries?"

"Just my pride, bro," Joe replied, wiping the mud off his visor. In the distance he could see their rival spinning "whoop-de-doos" on the trail, turning around the same axis in tighter and tighter circles. "What do you say we go catch that hot dog?"

Frank could hear the determination in his brother's voice, and he was concerned that Joe would push himself and his bike beyond their limits. Perhaps they were starting to take this competition too seriously. Up ahead, the rider had stopped and was waiting for them.

"Remember, we're just having fun," Frank cautioned. "Let's not take stupid risks, okay?"

"You bet," Joe answered. "Just having fun. Now, let's go!" As Joe mounted up, the rider waved them on. Instantly they were chasing along the trails again.

The rider raced away. The Hardys wound their engines past their redlines attempting to catch their new riding companion. Their engines screamed as the bikes flew through the air in tremendous powered leaps and hurdles. Within moments they were back on the straightaway running along the ridge. By then Frank had really begun to worry. The straightaway ended when a deep ravine cut right across the ridge at right angles. The ravine was over twenty feet across and more than fifty feet deep. Local riders called it Devil's Gap. If the rider up ahead was unfamiliar with the trail . . .

Frank kicked down one gear, dangerously overrevving his engine but gaining a burst of acceleration that finally brought him beside the stranger. He couldn't make out the newcomer's face behind the tinted visor, but he waved for his rival to stop.

The other rider ignored Frank's warning, gunning the engine of the fancy European bike and racing ahead. Directly ahead was Devil's Gap! Frank and Joe both veered off the trail, hoping their companion would do the same.

No—the other bike just rocketed forward. All the Hardys could do was watch in horror as the rider roared full speed toward the edge!

Chapter 2

THE BIG EUROPEAN MACHINE sailed over the edge of the ravine as the Hardys watched helplessly. They were certain that the bike's trajectory would end in disaster.

Then Frank saw that he was observing a true expert. Standing on the pegs of the bike, the person leaned back and pulled up on the handlebars to lift the front wheel higher. The bike seemed to soar over the ravine completely in control. It landed gracefully on the far side of the gap, its rear wheel touching down first, several feet from the edge. Feeling the contact, the rider gunned the engine, instantly regaining traction so that the bike shot smoothly forward. It was a perfect jump and a flawless landing.

Skidding to a stop on the other side of the ravine, the rider spun around to face the Hardys. One gloved hand flipped up the helmet visor to reveal the smiling face of Lindsey Nichols.

"What's the problem, guys?" she asked, laughing. "You're not afraid of a little ravine, are you?"

Frank and Joe gaped at each other, stunned that the rider was the girl who'd been flirting with Frank at lunch. They became determined. After all, this was their turf—they'd each jumped the ravine dozens of times. They whipped their bikes around, rode back far enough to get a good running start, spun around again and raced for the edge. At the last instant they each gave one more burst of throttle, hauled back on their handlebars, and went airborne.

The Hardys sailed over the ravine side by side and landed together in perfect sync. They pulled up hard on either side of Lindsey, who was clapping loudly. Frank flipped up his face shield.

"Well?" he said to her. "Are we riding, or what?" In response she took off down the trail, and the chase was on again.

As dusk settled over Hopkins Woods, Frank, Joe, and Lindsey idled their bikes in the clearing where the Hardys' van was parked. Beside it was a little red pickup with a narrow ramp lowered from its tailgate. Lindsey rode right up the ramp, settled her bike into braces built into the truck bed, and killed the engine. She pulled off her helmet and hopped out of the truck, ambling over to where the brothers were maneuvering their bikes into the back of the van.

"You're a great rider, Lindsey," Frank told her.

"Thanks—you're not bad yourself," she responded.

"But you were pretty foolhardy to take that jump," he added.

A flash of anger passed across Lindsey's face. "You and your brother took the same jump," she said. "What makes you so superior?"

"Hey, easy," Joe broke in. "Frank didn't mean to insult you. But we're familiar with these trails. We've done that jump before—"

"So have I!" she insisted. "Only an amateur rides blind. I came out here before you got here and checked out the course."

"Really? Where was your truck when we got here?" Joe said.

Lindsey stared down at the ground sheepishly. "I pulled into the woods when I heard you coming in," she said. "I wanted to surprise you." She met Frank's gaze. "Look, my dad taught me to take risks, but only when I understand the danger. I knew what I was doing."

"Your dad?" Frank asked quizzically, then

suddenly realized, "Hey—you must be Del Nichols's daughter. No wonder you're such a hot rider! He was the best competition rider this area ever produced."

"We bought our bikes at his shop!" Joe added.

Lindsey laughed. "And you guys thought I just wanted to come out here to watch you. Typical macho males. My dad taught me everything he knows about riding before I was twelve."

"You're right," Frank said. "If it's okay for us to take that jump, it's okay for you. You're as good a rider as we—"

"Better," she interrupted with a grin. "You two aren't bad, but you're not in my league."

"Hey, don't take too much credit," Joe protested. "Your bike has twice our horsepower. If we were on brand-new competition models like that—"

"You'd still get dusted by me," Lindsey said.

"Where have you been going to school?" Joe wanted to know.

"Away. But I waned to come back here for my senior year," Lindsey answered, making it clear she didn't want to discuss that any more. "If you really want to see if you can keep up with me on a bike, why don't you come out to the fairgrounds after school tomorrow?"

"The motorsports show!" Joe remembered. It was an annual event sponsored by Nichols's

Motorsports. Every fall, as motorcycle season gave way to snowmobile season, Nichols filled the Bayport Fairgrounds with displays, demo models, and accessories. The action highlights were the races on the fairgrounds track.

"There's a motorcross exhibition scheduled, and all the riders will be on bikes identical to mine," Lindsey said. "I can get you into the lineup. That way you won't have any excuses when I beat you again." She tossed her head and sauntered back to her truck. "See you tomorrow!" she called to them before she drove off.

"She doesn't have to worry about being too humble," Joe said to his brother.

Nearly twenty-four hours later, both Hardys were roaring around the motorcross course at the fairgrounds track, dicing for second place in a pack of a dozen racers. A crowd of onlookers was riveted to the action as the Hardys tried every trick they knew to catch the leader. They gunned their engines on the last lap, hurtled over the final jump, and pulled nearly even with Lindsey on either side. They were both less than a bike length behind her as she crossed the finish line, pumping her fist in the air.

A short, trim, middle-aged man bounded out of the crowd and rushed over to Lindsey in the winner's circle. He scooped her up in his arms and swung her in the air effortlessly and with surprising strength.

"Nice job, Lindsey!" he exclaimed. "It reminded me of the old days—when I was out there."

"Guess we should congratulate her," Joe muttered grudgingly as he and Frank parked their bikes.

"Guess so," Frank agreed. He couldn't help noticing how great Lindsey looked in her racing leathers. She was a bit taller than her father, about five-eight, long and lean. He remembered his promise to Callie the day before. Just friends, he reminded himself.

Lindsey spotted them and broke away from her father to take Frank's arm. "Dad, I guess you know Frank Hardy and his brother, Joe," she said. She whispered an aside to Frank: "Told you you couldn't beat me."

As Del Nichols shook Frank's hand he said, "I haven't seen you around the shop for a long time. Can I get you to come in and buy a couple of these?" he joked, gesturing toward the bikes they'd just raced.

"They're a bit out of our price range," Frank answered, smiling. "Besides, we don't really do all that much riding anymore."

"I'm sorry to hear that," Nichols said. "That was some fine riding from both of you."

"Thank you, sir," Frank responded. "Coming from you, that's a great compliment."

Del Nichols turned to Lindsey. "Have you asked them yet?"

Lindsey shifted uncomfortably. *"Dad,* I told you not to rush me. I'll get around to it."

She took both Hardys by the arm and started to lead them way. "Come on, guys, let's go for a walk. My father wants us to have a talk. Okay Dad?" she shot back at her father.

"You bet," he said. "Go have fun at the show. Don't let old Del stand in your way."

The trio strolled across the fairgrounds. It was a beautiful, cool autumn afternoon, and the sun cast long shadows among the exhibits and display booths. Joe saw plenty of merchandise he wished he could buy—everything from helmets, gloves, and jackets to the latest sport and touring motorcycles. He noticed Frank only had eyes for Lindsey and walked ahead to check some things out.

"So, why did you come back here?" Frank asked when Joe was out of earshot. He thought that maybe she'd talk to him without Joe around.

"Actually, I only lived here when I was very little, before my folks got divorced and I moved to Chicago with my mom. After that it was just summers—that is, summers when Dad wasn't too busy . . ." Her expression became more serious. "Anyway, I finally told my parents I wanted to live here instead of Illinois, and Dad surprised me by saying okay."

"Didn't your mother object to your moving out?" Frank wondered.

"I think she was secretly pleased. We were fighting a lot. We don't have all that much in common. I'm kind of a tomboy."

"I noticed," Frank put in dryly.

"You don't know the half of it," Lindsey replied. "I'm always looking for adventure. For instance, I spent this past summer alone, hiking in the wilds of Colorado."

"That's pretty impressive," Frank said.

"Yup," she said proudly. "I lived off the land. I found edible plants and mushrooms, and I kept a twenty-two rifle in my backpack for small game. I'm an expert shot—something else my dad taught me."

Frank gave Lindsey an admiring glance. He was amazed by how similar her go-for-it attitude was to his and Joe's. It wasn't often they ran into a girl like her.

"So, Lindsey, what did your dad want you to talk to us about?" Joe asked, rejoining them.

"I hate to ask you guys this . . . I mean, we've just met . . ." she hedged. "But did you ever hear of the Patriot?"

"It's a classic—the ultimate American road

machine," Frank said. "The last ones were made over thirty years ago."

"That's right." Lindsey smiled. "Except now some new ones might get built."

"I saw an article about it in a magazine a couple months ago," Joe said. "It said there was a rumor—"

"It's more than that," Lindsey interrupted. "You might not think it to look at him, but my father is a very wealthy man. He turned a successful racing career into a very successful business. His motorcycle dealership in Bayport is just one of several dozen bike and auto dealerships he owns in the Northeast.

"Anyway, recently he started looking for a legacy—something to invest in that would live on after him. He found the Patriot. Or at least, he found two men who each, individually, want to build brand-new ones. All each one needs is money."

"What does this have to do with us?" Frank asked.

Lindsey continued. "The problem for Dad is deciding who to back with his money. These two men used to be partners, and that was when they bought the rights to use the Patriot name. They never could agree on what kind of bike to build, so their partnership broke up. Each claims to own the rights, and they've been fighting it out in court. Whoever Dad decides to back will win out because they're both running out of money and the loser won't be able to afford to continue the ownership fight."

"That's pretty interesting," Frank said. "But I still don't see where we fit in."

Lindsey met Frank's eyes a bit sheepishly. "Well, when I mentioned your names to Dad, he perked right up. He says you're well-known detectives. He asked me to ask you to help him decide who to support."

"What does he want us to do?" Joe asked.

"Check out both companies and make a recommendation." She stopped and stood with her hands on her hips. "My dad doesn't know how to decide."

"Who are these guys, anyway?" Joe asked.

"I can introduce you to them," Lindsey said. "That's why I brought you here." She pointed to two separate booths, each with banners announcing the only genuine Patriot.

"There they are," Lindsey said. The Hardys could make out a shiny motorcycle in each display area, but the crowd around the booths blocked most of the view. Whoever Nichols had hired to lay out the show had accidentally placed the rivals side by side. Two beefy middle-aged men stood face-to-face, bellowing at each other like angry buffalos while the crowd egged them on.

"Hey, I know one of those guys," Joe told

Frank. "It's Lou Copeland." He tried to make himself heard over the hubbub, shouting, "Hey, Lou. It's me—Joe Hardy."

There was no response to Joe's greeting because the argument was really heating up. As Frank and Joe craned their necks to see over the crowd, the dispute suddenly exploded into violence, and the two rivals leapt at each other!

Chapter 3

THE TWO BIG MEN began pummeling each other on the head and shoulders. Copeland, slightly shorter than his opponent and about twenty pounds lighter, ducked under a sweeping haymaker and shot a straight right into the man's ample gut. The bigger man grunted and doubled over, wrapping his arms around Copeland.

They grappled clumsily, trying to hurl each other to the ground. They were already red faced and snorting when the Hardys shouldered their way through the crowd. Joe grabbed his friend, while Frank tried to break the other man's grip on Copeland.

"Lou, cut it out. Come on, back off!" Joe begged. Copeland didn't act as if he'd even noticed him yet. Joe grabbed Copeland around the waist, lifted him up, and swung him away from his enemy.

"Let me at him. I'm gonna kill him!" Copeland roared.

Meanwhile Frank had moved in front of Copeland's opponent, who began throwing wild punches. Frank dodged the punches easily, waiting for him to exhaust himself. When the big man began to wheeze, Frank gave him a little shove, making him sit down heavily on the ground. As his fury passed, he gazed up at Frank blankly, amazed and puzzled to find himself sitting in the dirt.

"You shoved me," he said.

Frank reached down and helped the man to his feet. "You were trying to punch me in the face," Frank said.

"Sorry—it wasn't you—I was trying to get at that traitor," the man snarled, glaring at Copeland.

"I'm the traitor? You're the one who broke up our partnership," Copeland growled back, straining against Joe.

"Let them fight!" a voice called from the crowd. Frank glanced over at its owner. He was small, wiry, and scruffy, in his late thirties, wearing biker colors. He stood next to an enormous, musclebound man about the same age, equally scruffy, and wearing similar clothes.

"You call this piece of garbage a Patriot?" the big biker yelled. "It's nothing but a fake."

Suddenly he whipped off a heavy chain from around his waist and whacked it down on the tank of Copeland's display bike, making a deep dent in the metal.

"I'll kill *them!*" Copeland howled, his rage redirected at the two bikers as they took off for the parking lot. Joe normally would have gone after the two bikers himself, but he was busy restraining Copeland.

"You're not going to kill anybody, Lou, so just calm down," Joe told him firmly. "They're already long gone." Copeland stared into Joe's face, finally recognizing him.

"Hey, Joe Hardy! How you doing, kid?" he said.

"The question is, how are *you* doing, Lou?" Joe responded. "What's going on here? You're not the kind of guy to get into a brawl."

"Ah, it's him—Ethan DeForrest! He just makes me crazy," Copeland answered, indicating his ex-partner, who was deep in conversation with Frank and Lindsey.

"I don't understand how two friends can become such enemies," Lindsey was saying to DeForrest. "What happened between you two?"

"He's just so blasted pigheaded!" DeForrest answered.

"How so?" Frank asked, taking hold of De-

Forrest's elbow and carefully leading him away from Copeland.

"Just look at that bike he built!" DeForrest exclaimed. "He thinks he can mass-produce the Minuteman. He's in over his head, and he wanted to force me to go the same route."

Frank glanced at Copeland's bike. "It looks okay to me," he said. "What's a Minuteman?"

Lindsey explained. "The Patriot company made two basic models, the Minuteman and a luxury rig called the Commander."

"I've read about the old Commanders—" Frank said.

"That's what I'm building," DeForrest interrupted. "Brand-new, modern luxury cruisers in the spirit of the old Commanders—"

"The Minuteman was smaller, lighter, sportier—" Lindsey continued.

"And cheaper," DeForrest said. "I wanted to keep production low and build a few high-quality machines. Copeland wants to try competing head-on with the big companies. It's crazy!"

Several yards away, Copeland overheard this outburst. "See?" he said to Joe. "He keeps insulting my business sense!" Joe knew that Copeland was a very successful businessman on a small, local scale. Copeland ran a performance shop and parts supply house. In addition to building fast custom bikes for the road and dirt, he supplied parts to owners of defunct or hard-to-find motorcycles. Many bike manufacturers had gone out of business over the years, especially British companies, and much of his business was mail-order, sending obsolete parts to riders and collectors all over the country.

Several years earlier Joe had been heavily into dirt bike riding, spending an entire summer successfully racing in amateur competitions. Copeland had offered to sponsor him if he wanted to turn professional. Although Joe ultimately decided to let riding take a backseat to detective work, the two had remained friends. Still, Joe hadn't seen Copeland for months.

"Come on, Lou," Joe said now. "Just because your partnership didn't work out doesn't mean that you and DeForrest have to punch out each other's lights. Why don't you show him you're the bigger man and apologize?"

Copeland grudgingly allowed himself to be led over to where Frank, Lindsey, and DeForrest stood. He held his hand out reluctantly. "Look," he said, "I guess we're stuck next to each other for the next few days. Why don't we make the best of it?"

With equal reluctance, DeForrest shook hands with his former partner. "I'll try to stay out of your way if you stay out of mine," he said.

As the Hardys and Lindsey walked off together, Lindsey said, "Thanks for cooling things off, guys. That could have turned really ugly. The thing is, they both have such good records. DeForrest is a successful businessman, too. In fact, he was one of the last Patriot dealers in the country, thirty years ago.

"They have completely different products and business plans, but both make sense. I don't know how Dad is ever going to choose between them."

"It's too bad they can't get back together and make both bikes," Frank said.

"Nice idea," Lindsey replied, "but each of them is convinced that the other's plan would lead to failure and ruin." She shook her head. "It's got to be one or the other."

"Well, maybe we can help make that decision after all," Frank said.

"Really? That would be great! I'm so glad we're going to be working together," Lindsey said, and threw her arms around Frank in a big hug. Frank smiled sheepishly as Joe frowned. There was no mystery involved here, just a business dispute. Why would Frank want to get caught up in that? Must be the girl, Joe decided.

After Lindsey left to tell her father that the Hardys had agreed to help out, Joe turned abruptly to Frank. "What are you thinking? Why do you want to get involved in this?" he asked.

"Just curious," Frank said. "Both those guys

could have real plans, or either or both could be complete frauds. Don't you want to find out?"

"I don't like the idea of spying on a friend," Joe said.

"You could be helping him out," Frank said. "Come on. Let's just go back there and ask them a few questions about their bikes."

Joe hesitated for a moment, then decided that his brother was probably right. What harm was there in asking a few questions?

Frank Hardy swooped through the cool night air, steering his middleweight sportbike along the curves of River Road. It was a clear, crisp autumn evening, and the ride was exhilarating. Frank followed the beam of his headlight in smooth, easy arcs. He loved the purring rumble of the bike's engine. As he rode he reviewed the events of the day.

While Joe had talked about old times with Copeland, Frank had gotten to know DeForrest a bit and found that he liked the man. DeForrest had invited him to come by to see his factory that night in Lakedale, some twenty miles from Bayport.

Soon Frank pulled his bike to a stop beside a building in a small industrial park on the outskirts of Lakedale. As he was flipping down the bike's sidestand, DeForrest came out of the front door to greet him.

"Frank—glad you could make it!" DeForrest said heartily. "Come on in, I'll show you around." Frank tugged his helmet off his head, shook hands with DeForrest, and followed him into the shop.

It wasn't a particularly large space, just a warehouse with an office off to the side, but it had been well set up. Bright fluorescent lights illuminated a sparkling clean, carefully laid out shop.

"See, I'm not thinking about mass production yet," DeForrest said. "Maybe four or five hundred units the first year, that's all. Each bike will be hand built at one of these workstations by a master mechanic, putting together one or two a week."

"What about parts?" Frank asked.

"Everything is farmed out to independent contractors," DeForrest explained. "I've designed the bike using the best equipment. The engine is a big V-twin, fifteen hundred cc's, eighty-five horsepower, built to my specifications. Come over here and I'll show you." He pulled a tarp off a gleaming motorcycle.

As DeForrest continued to describe the bike's selling points, Frank examined the machine closely. It was gorgeous. Patriot badges adorned either side of its shapely, sapphire blue gas tank, with the name *Commander II* in chrome script on the sidecovers. It had classic 1950s lines, but

Frank could see that its machinery was all modern and top quality—the stuff riders bought to upgrade their bikes' original factory equipment.

DeForrest's bike at the motorsports show was obviously a nonworking unit thrown together hastily. This was clearly the genuine article, the real prototype. "Does it run?" Frank asked.

"Listen," DeForrest said with a grin. He turned the ignition key, hit the starter button, and the big engine rumbled to life.

Frank couldn't help returning the man's grin. It was the sweetest engine note he'd ever heard, a deep, steady cadence with just the right hint of mechanical whir under the rumble. He imagined what it would sound like on the road, winding out to redline, then shifting to the next gear and winding out again.

Frank's revery was suddenly interrupted by the sound of breaking glass. A pane in one of the large windows that lit the shop during the day had been shattered and through it sailed a bottle with a burning rag stuck in its neck.

Thinking he might catch a glimpse of the assailant, Frank ran several feet to the window. In the dark he could barely pick out a figure in black road-racing leathers and a black helmet running away.

Meanwhile, the bottle had crashed to the cement floor. Within seconds there was burning gasoline spreading all over the warehouse floor!

Chapter 4

THE FIRE SPREAD RAPIDLY. Over the eerie crackle and pop of wooden crates catching fire, Frank could hear the note of a powerful motorcycle engine as it receded into the night.

"Frank, quick—grab that fire extinguisher!" DeForrest shouted. As DeForrest yanked a heavy extinguisher off the wall, Frank dodged flames and dashed across the warehouse floor to grab the second one.

A stack of burning crates off to Frank's left seemed to be the heart of the fire. He directed the stream of foam from his extinguisher into the stack, and the fire began to diminish. "I think it's out over here," Frank called to DeForrest.

"Good job—give me a hand over here," De-Forrest answered. "Some of these crates are as dry as tinder." DeForrest scurried among the lesser fires, putting out one, then another. Frank joined him. For several minutes it seemed that each time they extinguished one patch of flame, another sparked somewhere else.

When the last of the flames finally flickered and disappeared under a splash of foam, De-Forrest muttered, "I wonder if the bike's okay." He hurried over to the gleaming blue prototype. "Thank goodness," he said in relief. "Not a scratch!"

"The whole place seems to have come through pretty well," Frank said. He could hear the shriek of approaching fire engines. The flames must have set off an automatic alarm, he thought.

DeForrest surveyed the scorch marks all around him. "I don't know about that," he said. "I'm going to have to go through all those crates to figure out if any of my stock's been damaged." His face was a mask of anger. "It had to be Copeland, that sneaky dog! He's the only one who'd benefit if my place burned down." DeForrest turned to Frank. "Well, if he wants a war, he's got one."

"Whoa, take it easy," Frank said. "Let's not jump to conclusions." But the picture of that afternoon's brawl was still fresh in his mind.

With that kind of bad blood between Copeland and DeForrest, Frank could understand why DeForrest had decided his former partner was to blame.

At the same time, Lou Copeland and Joe Hardy were sitting across from each other in a booth at the Bayport Diner. "How's your burger?" Copeland asked. He picked at his salad, eyeing Joe's cheeseburger enviously.

"It's fine, Lou—you should have ordered one yourself," Joe responded. He took a big bite of the meaty sandwich.

"Wish I could, Joe, but my doctor would never forgive me," Copeland said. "I've got high blood pressure and high cholesterol, and he keeps telling me I'm twenty pounds overweight—this gettin' old's a pain in the neck."

"None of that stopped you from scrapping like a kid in a school yard this afternoon," Joe reminded him. "What were you thinking?"

"Guess I wasn't thinking at all," Copeland admitted. "DeForrest gets under my skin and I lose my cool. See, me and Eth'—that's what I used to call him when we were buddies—go way back. I started out as a mechanic in his old man's Patriot shop in Lakedale, back in the late fifties. Ethan took over the shop back around '61, when we were just out of our teens. He made a go of it until the factory shut down and there were no more new bikes to sell. I opened a little repair shop in Bayport after that, and DeForrest went into the appliance business. But we stayed friends, and we always talked about reviving the old bike."

"So what happened?" Joe asked around another bite of burger.

"We got our wish," Copeland answered. "Isn't there an old saying to be careful what you wish for 'cause you might get it? Well, that was us. We got it, then discovered we didn't have the same dream after all."

"The Minuteman-Commander dispute," Joe offered.

"Exactly," Copeland nodded.

"You couldn't work it out?"

"We couldn't work it out. No way. I'm not about to pour my heart and soul into building a few hundred fancy toys for rich yuppies who want to pretend to be big, bad bikers on weekends. I want to make a bike for anyone who's interested in owning a real, honest motorcycle without all the frills and plastic geegaws you get nowadays. Something anyone who loves bikes can appreciate—and afford." He became a bit sheepish, briefly turned his attention to his salad, then continued. "Sorry, kid, I got some passion about this, so I start making speeches soon as you give me the chance."

"I can understand," Joe said. "So how different are the bikes really?"

"Way different if you go by feel and style," Copeland explained. "Ethan's bike looks old-fashioned, what they call retro, I guess. My bike is clean and modern by comparison. His bike's a monster, over six hundred pounds. Mine's lean and mean, about four hundred pounds fully gassed and ready to go. Both engines are V-twins—wouldn't be a Patriot with any other engine layout—but mine revs higher, puts out about seventy horsepower from nine hundred cc's. I don't know how big his engine is, but it's huge."

He checked to see if Joe was following his explanation. "Look," Copeland continued, "they have the same differences as the original Patriots had. The Commander was the big power cruiser, the Minuteman the nimble, sporty one. In performance terms, there wasn't a whole lot of difference. Top speed, quarter-mile times, that stuff is all probably pretty close. But the intangibles—that's a whole different story.

"And now we've got a big problem," Copeland told Joe, and proceeded to fill him in on the legal battle over ownership of the Patriot name.

"Couldn't one of you just call your bike something else?" Joe asked, wanting Copeland's opinion. He didn't mention that Lindsey had already explained the situation.

"Sure, but the name's the whole point," Copeland responded. "People remember the Patriots. They were great bikes. There'll be a lot of excitement when new ones come out. If my bike's a Patriot, everyone in cycling will want to check it out. If it's some cockamamie name no one's ever heard of, then no one will care."

"If it's a good product it will sell," Joe said.

"Don't underestimate people's perceptions," Copeland told him. "With a good product, the name's worth millions of dollars. And that's what we're fighting for. But it's breaking both of us." Then he filled Joe in on Del Nichols's role in the drama, and once again, Joe kept quiet about what he knew and about his and Frank's involvement.

"Anyway, that's why I really wanted to talk to you," Copeland told Joe. "I think Del Nichols is leaning toward me, and I think Ethan knows it."

"So that's good, right?" Joe suggested, although he knew that Nichols was still undecided.

"Well, yes and no," Copeland responded. "Yes, it's good for my business. No, it may not be good for my health. See, I think DeForrest may try to kill me."

Joe was stunned. "Why do you think that?" he asked.

"Ethan's got a bad temper, worse than mine, and he's got some personal history. I told you that he went into the appliance business. But he also spent four years in state prison on a manslaughter rap." Copeland waited a beat to let this sink in before continuing.

"It was nearly twenty years ago—some guy pulled a knife on Ethan, and when it was over the guy was dead. See, he's had the experience of killing someone who got in his way—"

"That was a long time ago," Joe said. "And it sounds like he paid for the crime. I don't think you've got anything to worry about."

"You're probably right," Copeland answered. "But I figured you'd be a good person to talk to about this, you being a detective and all. So, you ready to go?"

"Gee, Lou, what about dessert? They make a great coconut custard pie here," Joe said in a deadpan.

"You're a real funny guy," Copeland said, reaching across the table to give Joe a playful shove. "Come on, let's get out of here."

Copeland stopped suddenly and gripped Joe's arm outside in the lit parking lot. "Look, kid, right now I'm all alone in this. Sure, I've got people lined up to work in my factory once I go into production. But they're just employees.

I could use someone to bounce ideas off, someone I can trust. I'd like to bring you in on this project, give you a title like security consultant or technical adviser. What do you say?"

Joe felt a twinge of guilt about not telling his friend that he and his brother were already committed to helping Lindsey and her father. How could he let Copeland confide in him, when that confidence could end up working against the man? But then he reassured himself that Copeland probably had the better product, and he already preferred Copeland's plan to mass-produce bikes for ordinary riders to DeForrest's scheme to build a few bikes for the wealthy. If he decided to recommend his friend to Del Nichols, he'd be doing Copeland a favor.

"I'd have to really believe in your bike, Lou," he told his friend. "So far I've only seen a mock-up. It looked nice, but—"

"Sorry, Joe," Copeland said. "No one's seen the prototype yet. In fact *I* built it to maintain security. It's not that I don't trust you. I just can't take chances showing it around yet. You understand, don't you?"

"I guess so," Joe said. On one hand, he could understand Copeland's concerns, but what if there really *wasn't* a prototype? That could easily explain his covering up, too.

Standing beside Copeland's pickup truck, Joe shook hands with his old friend and said, "I know this situation has got you pretty tense, Lou, but don't worry—it's all going to work out. I'll let you know what I decided."

Just then Joe heard a popping sound, like a small firecracker would make. Almost instantly the windshield of Copeland's truck blew out into what seemed like a million tiny pellets of glass.

Chapter 5

"GET DOWN!" Joe shouted to Copeland. "Somebody's shooting at us!" The older man froze for a moment, gaping at the shattered windshield. Joe finally popped up, grabbed his friend's shoulders, and shoved him down. They crouched silently on the pavement beside the pickup, waiting for another shot.

The next shot never came, but they did hear the roar of a motorcycle engine receding into the night. They stayed under cover for several moments more until Joe said, "I think the coast is clear."

Copeland got up slowly and walked around to the front of his truck to examine the shot-out windshield. Copeland shook his head as he surveyed the damage, then addressed Joe. "Still think I'm not in danger?"

Joe shook his head, too, then without answering went back inside the diner and placed a call to the Bayport Police. Within minutes Con Riley showed up with two other uniformed officers to question Joe and Copeland about the incident and check the scene for evidence.

"So it was just one shot?" Frank Hardy asked his younger brother. It was after eleven and the Hardys were sitting together in Frank's bedroom. Frank filled Joe in on the attack at DeForrest's factory, then Joe told Frank about the shooting in the parking lot.

"That's all," Joe said. "Lou was out there in the open for several seconds afterward, so if the shooter had wanted to put a bullet in him it should have been easy."

"It sounds to me like someone was just trying to scare him," Frank said.

"And they did a good job of it," Joe responded. "They dug a twenty-two round out of the upholstery of the driver's seat. Con said they'd check it out in the police lab, but—"

"That's the most common round in the world," Frank finished Joe's sentence. "There's not much chance they'll be able to trace it. What time did this happen?"

"Just after nine o'clock." Joe noticed his older brother's brow creasing as Frank went into what Joe liked to call his Sherlock mode. Frank was a master at analyzing situations and clues.

"It was about ten after eight when the arsonist hit DeForrest's shop," Frank noted. "If it was the same person, he'd have had less than an hour to get back to Bayport and take a shot at you. It's possible, but it'd be cutting things tight."

"And he would have to have known where we were," Joe pointed out. "Pretty good trick. At least we can rule out DeForrest and Copeland as the culprits, since we were with them."

"Which doesn't mean that your pal Copeland couldn't have hired someone to torch the factory and then shoot at him to divert suspicion from himself," Frank speculated.

"Wait a minute," Joe interrupted. "DeForrest could have done the same thing. How can you be so sure it was Lou?"

"Okay, fair enough," Frank admitted. "It could have been either of them. Or someone else entirely. In which case we'd need a whole new motive. I'll tell you one thing—I saw Ethan DeForrest's bike, and it's a beauty. Lou Copeland has reason to be worried."

"I wish I could tell you the same thing," Joe

said, "but Lou doesn't want to show me his bike. I'm not sure he even has one."

"That could be bad for his case," Frank pointed out.

"But I still believe in him," Joe said with more conviction than he felt. "If Lou Copeland says he has a bike, then I'll bet it's terrific."

"Could be," Frank conceded. "You know him better than I do. But one thing's for sure: we've got a mystery on our hands." He flashed a smile at his brother. "I hope you're happy."

"Well, I must admit," Joe said, "I'm not bored anymore."

It was almost two in the morning when Joe sat up in bed. Suddenly he was wide awake and wondering why. Then he heard what had awakened him—a motorcycle engine quietly idling outside. He climbed out of bed, moved silently to the window, and peaked out between the curtains.

Across the street, in the shadows just outside the circle of light cast by a street lamp, was a black motorcycle with a rider astride it. The bike's lights were off, and the rider wore a full-face helmet with a tinted visor. At this distance Joe couldn't tell the make, but the engine note was distinctive.

The rider seemed to be staring straight at Joe, who slowly pulled back one curtain to get a better look. The rider must have spotted the movement because he suddenly gunned the engine and took off. Halfway down the block he flicked on his headlight and roared off into the night.

An hour later Joe was still wide awake. Who was that rider in black? Was it the assailant who had shot at Copeland or tried to burn down DeForrest's factory? Maybe he and Frank were misreading the situation. Maybe *they* were the real targets. It was even possible that the rider was an enemy of theirs, someone who had nothing to do with DeForrest and Copeland. In that case it might only be a coincidence that he rode a motorcycle.

His mind poured over the possibilities, from the most likely to the most outlandish. He considered waking Frank but decided to let him sleep. He'd tell him about the rider later. Meanwhile it was Friday morning, and he didn't have to be at school for several hours. Rather than lie awake in bed, Joe decided to go watch the sunrise.

He dressed quietly in jeans, boots, and a sweatshirt. He grabbed his helmet, school books, and leather jacket, left a note for Frank taped to the bathroom mirror, and quietly made his way downstairs. Soon he was standing in the garage. The old dirt bikes were tucked away in one corner. His road bike, a middleweight cruiser-type machine, was parked next to Frank's sportbike. He stuffed his books into the leather saddlebags.

Joe opened the garage door quietly, eased his bike out, and rolled it down to the curb. Only then did he fire up the engine. He pulled on his helmet and tugged his gloves on, then he kicked the bike into first gear and took off.

Just maybe, Joe thought, the mystery rider was spending a restless night in the saddle. Maybe if he rode around, he would come across him. Maybe the other rider *wanted* to be discovered. Why else would he have idled the engine of his bike outside their house in the middle of the night? Perhaps it was the rider's way of saying "I know where you live and I'm watching you."

After nearly an hour roaming the empty streets, Joe began to doubt that he'd find the rider. At last he decided to watch the sunrise on the bluffs overlooking the bay. Joe was out of Bayport and in the country in less than ten minutes. The road was full of gentle curves, and there was no traffic at all yet.

The blackness of night began to give way to gray as Joe reached his destination. He popped the bike up on its center stand, yanked off his helmet, and lay back against the backrest with his feet on the handlebars. He gazed out across the bay, listening to the waves gently lapping at the shore below. Birds began to sing, and then the dawn broke, the sun rising and coloring the water blood red. It was going to be a beautiful day. Ah, that's more like it, Joe thought, and dozed off to sleep.

Two hours later, just after eight A.M., Joe woke up and glanced at his watch. He still had time to buy a doughnut and make it to homeroom on time. The morning sun felt warm on his face, and for a moment he allowed himself the luxury of imagining an all-day ride to somewhere far away. Instead he fired up his motorcycle and zoomed off for Bayport High.

"Hey, Frank, wait up!" a girl's voice called to him as he strode toward his locker. As Frank turned, Lindsey Nichols hurried up behind him. She latched on to his arm possessively and fell into step beside him.

"So what did the master detectives discover last night?" she asked.

Frank smiled back at Lindsey, but he was momentarily tongue-tied. She was wearing a pretty checked dress that stopped just above her knees. Frank had never seen Lindsey wear anything but her tough tomboy clothes, and the transformation was startling. She wasn't just pretty, she was beautiful.

"Actually, a lot happened last night," Frank said. "For instance, someone tried to kill us."

"What? You're kidding," she exclaimed, but

she could see that Frank was serious. "So tell me what happened."

Frank told her about the arson and about the shooting. When he was done, Lindsey took his hand in hers.

"I never imagined that we would be putting you and Joe in danger by asking for your help," she said earnestly. "Maybe you should just steer clear of Copeland and DeForrest and let my dad decide for himself."

"I don't think that's a good idea," Frank said. "Crimes have been committed. The guilty party has to be found and brought to justice. Besides," he added with a smile, "I'm not quitting this investigation until I get to ride the Commander."

"What about Copeland?" Lindsey asked. "Did Joe get to see his bike?"

Frank explained that he hadn't and that they suspected there might not even be a working Minuteman yet.

"Dad wants to make a decision soon," Lindsey said, "and if only DeForrest has a bike that works, that'll pretty much settle things. By the way, Frank, I really appreciate everything you've done for us," she continued, staring deeply into Frank's eyes. Lindsey paused, then pulled his face down to hers, wrapped her arms around his neck, and kissed him tenderly on the lips.

A movement down the hallway caught Frank's eye. He broke away from Lindsey and turned to see Callie Shaw standing several feet away, staring at the two of them with a stricken expression on her face. This was no friendly peck on the cheek Lindsey had given him, and his girlfriend had seen it all!

Chapter 6

BEFORE CALLIE TURNED AWAY, Frank watched tears start to flow down her cheeks.

"Wait, I can explain!" Frank called after Callie, who was stomping down the hall. As he broke away from Lindsey, she gave him a puzzled look.

"Who's that?" Lindsey asked.

"My girlfriend," Frank explained. "I'm sorry, Lindsey, I've got to go."

"I guess you do," Lindsey said, raising an eyebrow quizzically. "See you around."

Frank was close behind Callie. He anxiously called to her as he almost caught up, "Come on, Callie. Wait. I told you, Lindsey's just a friend. Joe and I are on a case for her and her father. You've got the wrong idea about this!"

Callie turned on him, and he took a step back. "Oh, do I?" she said. "And I'm supposed to believe that was just a friendly greeting?"

"She kissed *me,*" Frank protested.

"And you looked like you were really suffering there!" Callie said.

"I know what it looked like, Callie, but I didn't kiss her back. Look, can we talk about this?"

Just then the bell rang for the next class. Callie's expression softened slightly. "Not now," she told him. "I don't want to be late for class. I guess you deserve the benefit of the doubt—at least for now."

"Let's meet after school then—I'll buy you a slice of pizza," Frank suggested. He could see that Callie was wavering. "Look, it's an interesting case. I'll tell you all about it," he added, knowing that Callie considered herself a skilled amateur detective and that she couldn't resist the chance to become involved in one of his cases.

"Okay," Callie said. "But you'd better tell me all the details. And promise—no more passionate kisses with beautiful girls!"

"With one exception," Frank said. "You!" Callie hurried off to her English class and Frank headed for his physics lab. Actually he was troubled by Lindsey's kiss and his reaction to it. Frank barely knew the girl, but he did like her.

* * *

Joe Hardy fidgeted restlessly in his English class. Normally he'd be completely focused on Mr. Cramer, because the man brought books to life. Today Joe's mind kept drifting back to the events of the night before.

That bike outside the house was still bothering him. The sound of its engine intrigued him. He'd been around bikes for years, but he'd never heard that cadence before. It was similar to the "potato-potato-potato" cadence of a Harley. But it idled a bit faster and wound out way too high. He was pretty sure it was the same engine sound he'd heard after he and Copeland had been shot at earlier. He knew he'd recognize it if he heard it again.

"Well, Mr. Hardy, the whole class is waiting for your answer," Mr. Cramer was saying.

"Huh?" Joe grunted, realizing that the teacher was speaking to him. "I'm sorry, Mr. Cramer, I'm not sure I understood the question."

"That's all right, Joe, you seem to have been off on your own. When you come back to earth, let us know." The teacher turned to another student. "Ms. Maransky, what do *you* think?" Joe decided he'd better put all thoughts of motorcycles aside until after school.

That afternoon after school the Hardys sat in a booth at a pizza parlor in downtown Bayport, waiting for Callie. Frank had caught up to Joe in school earlier, and asked him to help explain things to Callie. Now, as they nursed their sodas, Joe told Frank about their late-night visitor.

"Why didn't you wake me?" Frank asked. "I was pretty surprised to find you gone when I woke up this morning. Mom, Dad, and Aunt Gertrude wondered where you were, too."

"There wasn't anything you could have done. The rider was gone. I just needed some time by myself to sort out my thoughts," Joe replied.

"Have you come up with anything?" Frank asked.

"Nothing new," Joe admitted. "What about you?"

Frank told Joe about Lindsey kissing him in the hall, and how Callie saw it all.

"Maybe you're getting a little too close to this case," Joe suggested.

"Don't I know it!" Frank replied. "Lindsey's getting under my skin. I like her a lot, but if I'm really in love with Callie, then I shouldn't have these feelings for someone else, right?"

"Hey, pal, Lindsey's gorgeous, and you two have a lot in common. Anyone would be attracted to her," Joe said. "But that doesn't outweigh what you and Callie have. You should think twice before doing anything to damage it."

Frank was surprised and a bit taken aback by

Joe's earnestness. He wanted to lighten things up. "Wow," Frank said. "And all this time I've thought of you as a complete neanderthal."

Joe grinned. "Yeah, well, don't spread it around. I have a reputation to maintain."

"Hi, guys," Callie said as she and Joe's girlfriend, Vanessa Bender, slid into the booth beside the brothers.

"Hey, you," Joe said to Vanessa with a smile.

"Hey, yourself." She grinned back at him. "Where've you been?"

"New case," he answered.

"Frank handed me the same line," Callie said. "We're here to learn all about it. Which one of you guys is going to start?"

"I will," Joe answered. "Pepperoni or mushrooms?"

"Both," the girls chimed in unison.

"Now talk," Callie insisted. Joe looked over at Frank, who took the cue and began to fill them in on the details of the case.

Sometime later, as the brothers finished their story and the four of them attacked their pizza, Vanessa said, "The whole thing sounds pretty fishy if you ask me!"

"How do you mean?" Frank asked.

"Well," Vanessa said, "why would either Copeland or DeForrest hire this rider in black to attack both his rival *and* himself? Why is it that these attacks didn't start until you two took on the case, and then they started right away?"

"Have you considered that you might be the targets, not Copeland and DeForrest?" Callie asked.

"We have, but that seems pretty coincidental, too," Frank answered.

"I think you guys are in over your heads," Callie said grimly. "You've walked into a very complicated situation without really knowing what's going on. Come to think of it, I wouldn't be surprised if your new 'friend' is using you somehow!"

"You mean Lindsey?" Frank protested. "She's just trying to help her father."

"Then they're *both* using you!" Callie said.

She was obviously a bit steamed about how fast Frank defended Lindsey. "We appreciate your concern, Callie," Joe added. "But there's really no reason for you to be jealous."

"I'm not jealous," Callie stated. "But I am suspicious. And you guys would be, too, if you weren't so dazzled by a pretty face!"

When the Hardys got home, they found a note from their mother on the refrigerator, reminding them that she and their father and Aunt Gertrude would be away for the weekend. They also got a message on their answering machine from Lindsey, asking them to meet her at her father's Bayport motorcycle dealership. There was a note of urgency in her voice.

It was just after six P.M. when the brothers rolled up in front of the dealership on their bikes. Nichols Motorsports, Inc., was housed in an enormous, one-story building. The showroom ran across the entire front of the building, its plate glass windows displaying scores of new bikes.

"Hey, guys, glad you could make it!" Lindsey bounded out of the dealership to greet them. She had changed from her school clothes to her jeans, boots, and T-shirt. She was wiping grease off her hands with a rag.

"I was just helping out in back," she explained. "There's an old Triumph that needed a gasket changed." The Hardys were impressed. Not only was she an expert rider but a mechanic, too.

"Dad's busy with a customer," she said. "He really wants to talk to you, but he asked me to show you around until he's free."

"Your message sounded urgent," Frank said. "Don't you want to tell us about it?"

"Dad made it very clear that he wants to do the talking," Lindsey answered, then quickly changed the subject. "When was the last time you guys were here?"

"It's been over a year," Joe said.

"Then there's a ton of new stuff," Lindsey said. "Want to take a look around?"

"Dad sells half a dozen different brands," she explained as they walked between the rows of shiny new bikes. "Since you guys were last here he's picked up two exclusive European makes. Of course, we've got all four Japanese brands and, as you know, they've got a dozen or more models each.

"All together we have over two hundred new bikes on the floor at any given time," Lindsey said. "And of course there are the seasonal vehicles—we've just moved the aqua skis out to make room for the snowmobiles—and then there are the power lawnmowers and snowblowers, generators, and all the accessories that go along with these products."

"We've always been amazed at how big this place is," Joe said.

After a few minutes Lindsey led them back behind the showroom, pointing out the offices, the parts department, the repair shop and, way in the back, the warehouse. Frank and Joe had never seen this area and were impressed by the huge inventory.

As they walked back from the warehouse, Lindsey peeked around the door of her father's office. He was still with his customer.

"I guess we've got a little more time to kill,"

Lindsey said. She and Frank began to talk, and Joe drifted down the hall.

He busied himself studying a case of trophies from Del Nichols's long, successful racing career. There were plenty of them, mostly for first-place finishes. Joe's attention was drawn to a group of photographs. One, nearly twenty years old, showed a victorious Del Nichols, in his mid-twenties, on the shoulders of four clean-cut young men—his pit crew. Joe guessed that at least two of them were in their teens when the picture was taken. Del's race bike was parked in the background.

At last Del Nichols finished with his customer and summoned them into his office. He shook hands with the Hardys.

"Thanks, fellas, I'm glad you could come by," he said. The friendly, open expression he'd worn for his customer had faded and was replaced by one of concern. "I think we've got a real problem," he said. "This arrived in today's mail. Take a look."

He handed them a note that was pieced together from newsprint. It read, "There will never be any new Patriots. If you try to finance either Copeland or DeForrest, something real bad might happen to you (and your pretty daughter). This is your only warning."

Chapter 7

DEL NICHOLS GAVE WAY to a burst of fury. "Nobody threatens me and my little girl!" he snarled. "Nobody!" He turned toward the Hardys. "You find out who's responsible for this threat! I'll kill him! I swear I will!"

"Easy, Mr. Nichols," Frank said. "You're not going to kill anyone. You know, we have good contacts in the Bayport Police Department. Their lab boys might be able to trace this note."

"Absolutely not!" Nichols said. "We start bringing the police into it and this nut will disappear and we'll never find him."

"The cops are already involved," Joe said. He told Nichols about the investigation of the shooting at the diner.

"Lindsey mentioned it," Nichols said.

"Let's hold off with the police for a while," Lindsey said. "Don't you think this will all blow over once we've made a deal with Copeland or DeForrest?"

Nichols addressed his daughter sternly. "Let me handle this." He turned to Frank and said, "Give it a couple of days before contacting the police."

Frank hesitated then gave in. "Okay, we'll see what we can find out," he said. "You know you have to consider the possibility that someone other than Copeland or DeForrest is responsible for what's going on. Can you think of anyone who'd want to wreck this deal for both of them?"

"Nobody comes to mind," he said, "but the note sounds like the work of a Patriot fanatic. Patriots were good bikes, but there are some folks who think they were the greatest things ever on two wheels. They're almost sacred. Someone like that could get real upset about a new version being made. It just wouldn't be 'pure' enough for him."

Joe recalled the scene at the fairgrounds. "Hey, Frank, that sounds like those two 'one-percenters' who were in the crowd when DeForrest and Copeland had their fight," he said.

"That's right," Frank said, and told Nichols about the two bikers. Motorcyclists often referred to outlaw bikers as one-percenters—the one percent of troublemakers who gave the other ninety-nine percent of law-abiding riders a bad name. Those two certainly fit the description, Frank thought.

Joe had another thought. He asked Del Nichols, "Does the Patriot engine sound similar to a Harley's?"

"Yeah, but a good ear can tell the difference," Nichols said.

Now Joe told Nichols about the engines he'd heard the night before in the parking lot and in front of his house and his suspicion that they were from the same bike. "My guess is that it was a Patriot," Joe said.

"Makes sense that a Patriot fanatic would own a Patriot," Del Nichols said.

"And anyone who owns an old bike will eventually need parts for it, right? Hard-to-find parts," Joe continued.

"What are you getting at, Joe?" Lindsey asked.

Frank picked up Joe's line of reasoning, "And who's the biggest supplier of parts for classic bikes in this area?"

Both Lindsey and Del Nichols paused for a beat, then said in unison, *"Lou Copeland!"*

By eight that evening the Hardys' bikes were parked outside Lou Copeland's. On Friday nights Copeland stayed open till nine, so he was still inside going over the receipts when Joe and Frank walked in.

"Well, I've got a number of customers who own Patriots," Copeland mused after they explained why they were there. "I'd say there are about a dozen of them still running in the Bayport area."

"What about those two outlaws at the motorsports show?" Joe asked.

Copeland stared at him blankly.

"Come on, Lou, you must remember them," Joe encouraged him. "The ones who messed up your prototype."

Copeland frowned. "Joe, I was so steamed when that happened I hardly saw who it was who did it. Wait a minute—were they real outlaw types?" Joe nodded, and Copeland continued. "Was one a little, scrawny, nasty-looking fella and the other one a big moose?" Joe nodded again. "Alvie Moore and Rhino Riordan," Copeland said with authority.

"You know them?" Frank asked.

"Oh, yeah, we go way back," Copeland said. "A pair of middle-aged hoods still reliving their greaser teens. They ride with the Sinners."

The Hardys knew the reputation of the Sinners. They were a notorious biker gang who were always in trouble with the law.

"They could be the ones who sent the letter

to Del Nichols," Frank said. "Do you think they're dangerous?"

"Those two are as crazy as they come," Copeland answered. "I'd say they're capable of almost anything. In fact, I'll bet they're the ones who took that shot at us, Joe. Come on, guys, I know where they hang out—at the Sledgehammer. Let's go talk to those slimeballs." Copeland leapt out of his chair.

"Whoa, hold it, Lou!" Joe said. "Am I going to have to calm you down every time we get together? We don't even know if these are the guys. They're suspects, that's all. We just want to talk to them now."

"And we're much better off doing that by ourselves, without you along flying off the handle," Frank said. They left after a mild protest from Copeland. He calmed down when Joe promised to keep him informed.

"So this is the place, huh?" Joe asked. He and Frank sat in their van, Frank at the wheel. They were parked in the roughest part of town, around the corner from a seedy bar called the Sledgehammer. This was where the Sinners hung out.

After they'd left Copeland, the Hardys went home to pick up their van. Copeland had suggested that the Sledgehammer would be a good place to start. Now that they were here, they were unsure what to do next.

A long line of bikes was parked in front of the place, and loud rock music blared out from inside. Every once in a while a shriek of shrill female laughter pierced through the shouts, hoots, and jeers of harsh male voices. The Sledgehammer was a very rowdy joint, and the Hardys knew they would have to be careful.

"We don't even know if Alvie and Rhino are in there," Frank said. "And I don't think barging in and asking for them is a good idea."

"No kidding," Joe said. "They probably pound heads for fun. Why don't we get out and take a look around," Joe suggested. He started up the van and pulled it to within a few yards of the lineup of motorcycles. The brothers climbed out cautiously.

There were more than twenty bikes in all. Most of them were "choppers," customized with raked-out front ends, tall handlebars, low seats, spindly front wheels, and massive, fat rear tires. Some of these bikes were gleaming, show quality pieces with glittering metallic paint jobs and highly polished chrome all over. Others were "rat bikes," so beat up and encrusted with grime that the Hardys wondered how they ran. But they knew that such bikes were considered a personal statement, and that the dirt often masked perfectly maintained engines and mechanical parts.

They walked slowly past the row of bikes, checking out each machine. Most were Harley-Davidsons, some brand-new, some as old as forty years. A few were Indians, another long-gone classic American brand. There was a handful of old British bikes scattered among the pack—two Triumphs, a Norton, an immaculate, completely stocked BSA. These, too, were brands that were no longer in production.

"These guys sure do love their antiques, don't they?" Frank said.

"A lot of guys think modern bikes are too perfect," Joe explained. "They think the new Japanese and European bikes work so well that they're more like appliances than motorcycles. No soul. They like old bikes they can fiddle with."

Frank stared dubiously at a couple of the rattier choppers. "It's hard to see how some of these bikes have been improved."

Joe knew that his brother was a fan of high-tech. The more modern, complicated, and slick a machine, the more Frank loved it. Joe understood the value of simpler, more traditional styles as well as that of modern machines. He supposed that was why he rode a laid-back cruiser, while Frank owned a high-intensity sportbike.

Now Frank peered more closely at the pair of rat bikes he'd just noticed. "Hey, Joe, take a look at these," he called softly.

Joe joined Frank, who was now kneeling by the two bikes. "They're definitely not Harleys of any vintage," Frank said. "Even though they have V-twin engines."

"They're not Indians, either," Joe said. "Guess what? They're Patriots, the only ones in the whole line." He looked even more closely at the two machines. One was considerably larger than the other. "This one's an old Commander," he told Frank. "Probably dates from the early fifties. The other one's a Minuteman, seven or eight years newer. I think we've found what we were looking for."

"Isn't that nice," a gruff voice said from behind them. "And we've found you!"

Frank and Joe spun around to find themselves facing a mob of nearly a dozen angry-looking bikers. The leader, a shaggy, medium-size man, wore a leather vest over his bare chest, revealing enormously muscular shoulders and arms covered with tattoos. The other bikers came in an assortment of shapes and sizes—all big and all intimidating.

The leader pointed at the Hardys' black van. "We don't like it when young punks start sniffing around to steal our bikes," he snarled.

Chapter 8

"WE'RE NOT STEALING anyone's bike!" Joe protested.

"Yeah, right—you're just window shopping," the leader mocked. "It happens all the time—some punk cruises by and tries to stuff one of our bikes into a van. But we caught you this time!" The leader and several other bikers began to move toward the Hardys.

"Wait!" Frank said, holding up his hand. "Look, guys, we just want to talk to the owners of these two Patriots!"

Now Alvie Moore and Rhino Riordan shouldered their way to the front of the pack. "They're not for sale, kid," Rhino rumbled, and the other bikers chuckled ominously.

"We're not buying," Frank said. "We just want to talk."

"All right, so, talk," Alvie said. "*Then* we'll stomp you!" More laughter from the bikers followed.

"Lou Copeland said we might find you two here," Joe said.

"You guys know Lou?" Alvie muttered. "Lou's all right. At least he used to be until he started showing that piece of junk he calls a Patriot."

"Well, he thinks highly of you, too," Joe told Alvie. He took a step closer to the small biker and loomed over him. Joe wanted Alvie to understand what he'd be up against if there was a brawl. "In fact, Lou wants me to ask if you're the guy who took a shot at him last night."

"Who would be stupid enough to take a shot at Lou Copeland?" a red-bearded biker exclaimed. "Who would we get parts from if he were dead?" Several others grunted their agreement.

"You hear that?" Alvie told Joe through gritted teeth. He took a step back from the younger Hardy. He was twice Joe's age, but Joe was a lot bigger and in better shape. "Why would I take a shot at Copeland?"

"Because you hate the idea of new Patriot bikes being made and you'll do anything to stop them," Frank said. "And that includes threatening Del Nichols and his daughter."

Rhino Riordan shoved his way toward Frank. "We don't have to listen to this garbage," he bellowed. "Let's kick their heads in!" The bikers surged forward. Joe and Frank dropped into defensive stances, standing back to back. Here it comes, Joe thought.

But then the leader of the biker mob stepped between them and the Hardys. "Hey, brothers, let's settle down," he told them. "You gotta admit, these guys have some brass to come *here* and accuse Alvie and Rhino." He turned to the Hardys. "Okay, guys, that was good for a few laughs. Now get out of here before you get hurt."

Frank could see that Joe was starting to heat up, especially since he didn't like being taken lightly. But this wasn't the time or place to show how tough they were. He grabbed his younger brother by the arm and said, "Come on, Joe, let's go. We're not going to get anything out of these guys."

"But . . ." Joe started to protest, then thought better of it. "Right," he said. The odds were just stacked too heavily against them. They went back to their van, got in, and drove off. One of the bikers, probably disappointed that a fight never developed, tossed a bottle at them. Frank caught a glimpse of it in the rearview mirror as it smashed into the pavement behind them.

They didn't plan to go far. Frank followed a loop back through some side streets and parked again a few blocks from the Sledgehammer. The brothers climbed out of the van, threw open the back doors, and rolled out their road bikes. They locked up the van, fired up their engines, rode back to the Sledgehammer, and parked the bikes in a little dead-end. From there they could see the front of the Sledgehammer, but they couldn't be seen. Joe glanced at his watch. It was past eleven o'clock. Good thing their parents were away and it was Friday night, he thought, because it looked as if it was going to be a long night.

Minutes turned into an hour, then two, as they waited. For much of the time they were silent, each brother deep in his own thoughts. Every once in a while one or more of the bikers would drift out, saddle up, and ride away, but so far there had been no sign of Alvie or Rhino.

When the two Patriot riders finally left the club there were fewer than a dozen bikes out front.

"There they are," Frank whispered.

"I see them," Joe grunted. "If they split up I'll take the little guy."

Frank gave him a stern gaze. "Don't go looking for trouble."

"Whatever you say, Frank," Joe answered flatly.

Alvie and Rhino swung their legs over their old beat-up bikes and fired them up.

"Does that sound like the bike you heard last night?" Frank asked.

"They're more similar than anything I've heard, but not quite right," Joe said. "I think the Minuteman is closer." Then he fired up his own bike. There was no more time to talk if they didn't want to lose the bikers.

The Hardys leaned their bikes into the turn as they pulled out of the dead end. They kept the taillights of the two Patriots up ahead in sight but were careful not to get too close as they followed in the darkened streets of Bayport. In a seedy district on the outskirts of town, Alvie and Rhino split up. The Hardys had anticipated this, which was why they brought their bikes instead of the van. Now Joe veered off to follow Alvie, while Frank stayed with Rhino.

Rhino's route soon led out of Bayport onto the curving river road to Lakedale that Frank had followed yesterday. The big man's riding skill impressed Frank. Rhino was on a forty-year-old machine that looked as if it was ready for the junk heap, yet Frank was working hard on his modern sport bike just to keep the guy in sight.

Frank wondered why Rhino would be heading for Lakedale this late at night. Was he going to make another attempt on Ethan DeForrest's business? He thought back to the attack the past night and his brief glimpse of the arsonist. It might have been Rhino or Alvie, but he doubted it. Outlaw bikers hated helmets. Even when they were forced by law to wear them, they chose the smallest helmets possible. Often those were hardly more than fiberglass beanies. But the arsonist last night wore a full helmet with a blacked-out faceshield. And the rider Joe saw outside their home was wearing black, full racing-style leathers in addition to the visored type of helmet. The Sinners and their like tended to wear ragged jeans over engineer boots, T-shirts, and leather or denim vests with their club's "colors" emblazoned on the back. On cooler nights, like tonight, Alvie and Rhino wore their denim vests over beat-up leather jackets. Nothing that they wore was like the fancy racer-style garb of the mystery rider. Frank wondered if Rhino would change his clothes before striking out at DeForrest. On him, racing leathers and a full helmet *would* be an unexpected disguise.

The curves in the road tightened. Frank had to push harder to keep Rhino in sight. He couldn't afford to get so close that the big biker was in constant view. Occasionally, Frank let Rhino disappear around a corner, then when a lazier turn or a long straight opened up, his taillight would come back into sight. Frank was still astonished at how fast the big biker was taking this difficult road, lit only by a weak headlight and the light of the three-quarter moon.

Suddenly Frank realized that he'd swooped around several bends in the road, and Rhino had not come back into view. Frank doubted the old Patriot was capable of producing a big enough burst of speed to disappear that quickly. He'd lost his prey, though, so Frank yanked back on the throttle, and his bike shot forward.

Now Frank was riding near the peak of his ability and if Rhino was up ahead Frank was sure he'd catch him. Frank was leaning so far into some of the turns that he nearly scraped his knee on the pavement. He roared down the river road for several miles, but there was no other traffic. Where was Rhino?

Then, in his rearview mirror, Frank spotted the single beam of a motorcycle's headlight. He eased up on the throttle, hoping to catch a glimpse of the rider, and the headlight behind him quickly grew in size and brightness as the other bike closed in. He glanced over his left shoulder. Sure enough, it was Rhino Riordan. He must have spotted Frank tailing him, turned off his lights, then pulled off to the side of the road. Frank must have blasted right by without seeing him. Frank had quickly gone from being the hunter to the hunted.

Once again Frank cranked back on his throttle. Every time he entered a curve now, he was on the verge of wiping out. Not only was Rhino Riordan keeping up, he was gaining. Frank realized that under the dirt and grime was concealed a highly modified engine, with much more horsepower than the original motor.

Rhino was coming up on Frank very fast. When Frank glanced over his shoulder again, Rhino was barely two bike lengths behind. Frank made out a startling image in the moonlight—the biker's face was contorted in a furious half-smile, half-snarl. His right hand was holding the throttle of his old bike wide open, and his left was whirling a heavy chain over his head. He was preparing to whip Frank with it as soon as he caught up!

Chapter 9

AS THE BIG BIKER drew abreast of Frank he lashed out with the chain, swinging viciously at Frank's helmet. Frank ducked, and the blow passed harmlessly over his head. But he saw the murderous gleam in Rhino's eyes and knew he might not be so lucky next time.

Frank realized that his only chance lay in the superior combination of power and handling of his more modern motorcycle. He cranked back hard on the gas and his bike shot forward. He glanced down at the speedometer—he was going far too fast for this road at night, but he had little choice if he wanted to survive.

Now the gap between the two bikes opened up to one bike length, then two, then three.

Frank could see Rhino in his rearview mirror. The Patriot rider had slung his chain around his neck and now had both hands back on the bars of his bike. Slowly Rhino began to close the distance again.

Then, as he whipped around an especially tight turn, Frank suddenly lost all control over the situation. A flash of headlights momentarily blinded him. It was a car, approaching at high speed. It looked gigantic and seemed to fill the narrow road.

Frank had one instant to react before he'd be squashed like a bug. He swerved to avoid the big sedan, causing his brakes to lock up. Skidding off the pavement, his bike slid onto some gravel on the shoulder, the tires scrambling for a grip. He wrestled with the handlebars, trying desperately to stay upright.

It was hopeless. The bike bounced off the shoulder, launching Frank into the bushes and weeds along the roadside. He only had time to think that he wouldn't be hit by the car. And then he was airborne, flying over the handlebars. He came down hard enough to drive the air out of his lungs. It felt as if something in his chest crumpled as he hit.

Somewhere off to the right he could hear his bike crashing into a big tree. He struggled to stay conscious. The last sound he heard before everything went black was Rhino's bike receding into the night.

Joe Hardy banked his bike around another corner. Despite the fact that he was on a case, trailing a suspect, he was enjoying the ride. It was a crisp, cool night, and the streets of Bayport were nearly empty. Alvie Moore was close enough so Joe wouldn't lose him, but far enough not to know he was being tailed.

There was a special pleasure in riding through town late at night. The streets were empty, except for an occasional car or van.

Joe wondered how his older brother was doing, and where Rhino would lead him. He also wondered where his own quarry was taking him. They were motoring through a part of town Joe had never seen at night. It was a warehouse district, with many dark alleys and dead ends.

At last Alvie cut his engine and coasted to a stop. Joe cruised past him and continued on for several blocks before turning onto a side street. He made his way back to within a block of where the wiry little biker had pulled over. Joe cut his engine and glided to a stop. He parked his bike, hung his helmet on the mirror, and jogged silently back to where he'd last seen Alvie Moore.

Glancing around, Joe realized he was in familiar territory, the corner of Maple and Thorndyke—the corner of Lou Copeland's warehouse, where the bulk of his stock was kept. Back when he was racing competitively, Joe had been there a couple of times. Alvie's Patriot was parked out front. But where was Alvie?

On the Maple Street side of the warehouse there was an alley running between it and the next structure. Joe remembered that the loading ramp, as well as a side entrance, was on that side of the building. If Alvie was in there he'd be hidden from view.

Joe eased his way along the warehouse until he came to the alley. He cautiously peered around the corner. A single, exposed lightbulb hung over the loading ramp, and by its feeble light he could make out a figure hunched in front of the side entrance. It was Alvie.

Joe turned into the alley. Silently he began to approach the small biker, who seemed to be fiddling with the lock on the door. Why was Alvie trying to break into Copeland's warehouse? He decided the best way to find out was to use the direct approach.

Joe was just a few feet away when he whispered sharply, "Hey, Alvie, what are you doing?"

Alvie was taken completely by surprise. He whirled, fumbling a shiny metal object that fell jangling to the ground at his feet.

"You—you're one of the kids from outside the Sledgehammer," he wheezed. "What are you doing here?"

"I could ask you the same question," Joe said. "Looks like I caught you trying to break into Lou Copeland's warehouse. The way I see it, either you're planning to steal something or wreck something." He gave Alvie a conspiratorial smile. "So which is it, Alvie?"

Alvie smiled back at Joe. "Nah, you got it all wrong, pal," he said as he took a step toward Joe. He raised his hands in a conciliatory gesture.

"Then what's your explanation?" Joe asked.

"See, it's like this . . ." Alvie said. He clapped his hands and took another step closer. Startled, Joe pulled back, but Alvie let loose a vicious kick that caught Joe just under the right knee.

Joe's leg buckled with sudden, searing pain, Alvie had steel-toed boots. A little higher and he might have shattered Joe's knee. As Joe fell, Alvie was all over him, throwing hard lefts and rights at his head. Joe regained his balance, trying to ignore the sharp pain in his knee. He covered up, blocking most of Alvie's blows with his forearms. But one or two slipped by, catching him around the temples. He was dazed, taken aback by how hard the guy could punch.

As he battered Joe, Alvie snarled, "You mess

with me, kid, you get messed up. This'll teach you to stay out of my way."

Joe knew he was in trouble. He was up against an expert street fighter with nearly thirty years experience in dirty tactics. Joe outweighed this guy by nearly fifty pounds, but he was still going to lose the fight if he didn't do something fast.

Joe forced himself up, despite the pain that ripped through his knee. "That's enough!" he bellowed. "Now it's *my* turn!"

Driving in through Alvie's flurry of blows, he grabbed the smaller man under the armpits and hurled him across the alleyway. Alvie crashed into some empty garbage cans, scattering them, and popped right back to his feet.

By now Joe had regained his composure. He remembered the lesson his karate master taught him about dealing with street fighters.

"A street fighter is all wild attack," his *sensei* had said. "Let him get you off balance and he can overwhelm you. But once you gain control of the situation you can pick him apart one punch at a time. Keep your head and you will win. But remember to expect the unexpected."

As Alvie attacked again with his wild punches, Joe coolly sidestepped and caught him with a straight, hard jab to the jaw. The punch staggered Alvie, and Joe followed it up with a right cross that knocked him reeling and a left hook to the ribs that crumpled him. Alvie went down on one knee, gasping for breath. Joe smiled inwardly. Once again, the lessons about hand-to-hand combat his *sensei* taught had saved him.

"Okay, okay, that's it," Alvie gasped. He held out his right hand as Joe limped in to finish him off. "I give up, kid. Can you give me a hand?" Joe hobbled over and reached down to help him up.

Suddenly Alvie's helpless expression turned to one of pure venom. He lashed out with his left hand, and Joe felt a sudden, ripping pain. He glanced at his right arm. The sleeve of his leather jacket was slashed cleanly, and blood was beginning to ooze through the tear. Joe couldn't believe he'd let this evil little biker sucker him again. Too late, he heard his teacher's voice, this time warning against overconfidence.

Joe reeled back as Alvie slashed at him again. This time Joe saw the murderous little biker's weapon clutched in his left hand—it was a deadly straight razor.

Chapter 10

"I'VE HAD IT WITH YOU, PUNK," Alvie growled, wiping a trickle of blood from his nose with his right hand. "You messed around where you don't belong once too often. Now you're dead!"

Joe jumped back as Alvie slashed at him again with the straight razor. Joe tried to concentrate on the threat, suppressing the pain his arm and his knee. He knew that a razor could be even more dangerous than a knife because of its incredible sharpness. It was clear to Joe that his opponent was an expert with this deadly weapon, too.

Joe and Alvie circled each other warily. When the biker lunged forward once more, Joe bent down and scooped up the lid of one of the metal garbage cans Alvie had scattered in his fall. Holding the lid by its handle, Joe blocked Alvie's slash, then punched hard with the lid, catching Alvie full in the face. The trickle of blood from the biker's nose became a spouting stream, which he tried to stop by clutching his face with his right hand.

"Aaargh! You broke my nose!" Alvie cursed as he reeled back in pain.

Joe moved in to finish Alvie off, but his leg buckled as a stabbing pain shot through his knee.

Alvie saw his chance. He ducked around Joe and made a dash for the alley entrance as the younger Hardy struggled to stay on his feet. Joe tried to chase him but could only manage a painful hobble. In a moment Joe heard the biker's Minuteman fire up and roar off. Sighing with relief, Joe leaned against the wall of the warehouse. He slid down into a sitting position to examine his injuries.

He peeled off his jacket gingerly, fearing what he might find. To his relief, he discovered that the thick leather had protected his arm from serious damage. There was a long, shallow gash running across the top of his forearm, but the blood from the wound had already begun to congeal. Next he pulled his jeans up over his right knee. Between the top of his riding boot and his knee was a big purple bruise, swelling up like a robin's egg. He touched it and winced. It hurt like crazy, and he thought he might be limping for the next couple of days, but he was pretty sure that nothing was broken.

Joe chided himself for underestimating his enemy. Because Alvie was small, Joe had assumed he was no threat. It was a lesson he wouldn't soon forget. The little biker had turned out to be one of Joe's toughest opponents. He wanted a rematch.

Joe pulled a small, powerful flashlight from his pocket, stood up, and limped over to the warehouse door. He shined the light around on the ground, looking for whatever it was Alvie had dropped. Joe guessed that the biker was using some sort of pick to jimmy the lock. His light glinted off metal and he bent down to pick up a shiny new key.

Now Joe's curiosity was really aroused. He tried the key in the lock on the warehouse door. It slid in easily and with a little fiddling, it turned. The lock popped open. Now Joe was really puzzled. Alvie hadn't been breaking in—he was letting himself in. Why did Alvie Moore have a key to Lou Copeland's warehouse?

Joe gave a gentle tug, and the door swung open. He slipped inside. The warehouse seemed like a big, dark cavern. The beam from his little light cut through the shadows as Joe played it over the shelves of merchandise.

There were thousands of separate items stored here. Joe wondered what Alvie could have been looking for, or if he had just come to do as much mischief as possible. Maybe he just wanted to help himself to some free parts. Joe continued to examine the contents of the warehouse. Around a wall of shelving he found a line of old, worn-out motorcycles. They were a battered lot, some of them stripped of most of their parts, others almost complete. Then he noticed one that didn't seem to fit, at the end of the line.

Joe hobbled over to the bike, and whistled softly when he realized what it was. It was the Minuteman prototype! Bright red, gleaming with chrome highlights, the bike was absolutely gorgeous, far more beautiful than the mock-up displayed at Copeland's booth at the motorsports show. So this was what Alvie was after, he guessed. If the biker had found this bike, Joe surmised, he would have either stolen or damaged it. Now Joe was pretty certain that it was Alvie and Rhino who were conspiring against Lou Copeland. Maybe they were working for Ethan DeForrest after all, and the firebombing of *his* warehouse was just set to direct suspicion away from him. That didn't make sense unless he was certain that the fire wouldn't do much damage. And there was still the problem of the key. . . .

Joe found a light switch, flicked it on, and the warehouse was instantly illuminated by the glow of fluorescent lights. He spotted a phone on an old wooden desk in the corner of the warehouse. He fumbled in his pocket for a number he'd scribbled on a scrap of paper, then dialed.

"Lou, this is Joe Hardy," he said when a bleary Copeland answered. "I'm at your warehouse, and I just had a run-in with one of those bikers. . . ." Joe proceeded to tell Copeland about his encounter with Alvie Moore and about Alvie's key to the warehouse.

Frank Hardy woke to find himself sprawled in a mass of weeds several dozen yards from where he had been run off the road. He lay on his back, trying to recall exactly what had happened. Gradually he began to flex his fingers, then his toes. So far, so good, he thought. He tried bringing his arms gently to his sides, then drew his knees up. He rolled his shoulders slowly and carefully, and only then did he try, ever so cautiously, to move his head.

Nothing was broken, it seemed. He ached everywhere, but, almost miraculously, he was relatively uninjured. He rolled over onto his side, and a sharp pain shot through his ribs. Well, maybe there was some damage after all, he thought. He probed his side with his fingers until he found the injury. No, not as bad as it could have been. Maybe his ribs were cracked, but he'd had enough football injuries to be pretty certain he was okay. Moving slowly and carefully, he struggled to his feet.

He took inventory of where he hurt the most. The ribs on his right side were bruised. His right shoulder was sore. When he stepped down on his right foot, pain shot through his ankle. "Guess I took the hit on my right side," he told himself. He realized that the thick weeds had softened the impact, but still, Frank was thankful that he wore full leathers and a helmet. They were state of the art, with Kevlar and foam armor in strategic places, just like the top racers wore. And like those racers, he had survived an accident that would have seriously injured or killed an unprotected rider.

His bike's headlight was still shining and its beam cut at a funny angle up through the night. He made his way to the machine, which was lying on its side, the front end twisted from its impact with a tree trunk. The tree had gouged a huge chunk out of the bike's fiberglass bodywork, and its windshield was smashed. Frank gripped the handlebars and slowly wrestled the four hundred and fifty-pound machine back into an upright position. He tried the starter button, and the bike fired right up.

Not too much later, Frank Hardy guided the bike to a sputtering halt in front of Ethan De-

Forrest's building in Lakedale. He hadn't exceeded thirty miles per hour the entire trip back, and even so the front end wobbled dangerously. Ethan DeForrest came jogging out of his factory to greet Frank.

"Hey, Frank, I wish you'd let me come for you with the company van," he said as he helped him off the battered machine. Frank had found a phone box near where he'd crashed and called DeForrest at home. He'd refused DeForrest's offer of help and warned him to expect trouble from Rhino Riordan. He suggested that DeForrest go protect the factory, and promised to meet him there. Now, as DeForrest helped Frank inside, the older man continued, "Are you sure you're okay?"

"Yeah, just bashed up a bit," Frank assured him. "No sign of Riordan?"

"Not yet," DeForrest noted.

"Do you know these guys?" Frank asked.

"Tell me their names again," DeForrest said.

He listened carefully as Frank described the two one-percenters. DeForrest shrugged and said, "Sorry, Frank, they're strangers to me. You're pretty certain these are the people trying to stop the Patriot project?"

"Projects," Frank corrected him. "They seem to be after Copeland, too. And the Nicholses."

DeForrest suggested that part could be for appearances, and Frank agreed.

They waited together for almost an hour, but when no threat materialized, DeForrest finally said, "Why don't you go home and get some rest? I've got a cot in my office—I'll stay here until morning to make certain there's no trouble."

Frank argued halfheartedly but allowed himself to be persuaded. He started toward the front door where his bike was parked, but DeForrest stopped him. "You can't ride that. Leave it here and I'll take care of it. I've got something out back you can use."

Joe Hardy paced impatiently around his bike, which was parked beside the black van, wondering where his older brother was. It was an hour past their designated meeting time, and there was no sign of Frank. It would be dawn in another couple of hours, and he was exhausted and irritable. He was pretty banged up, and he just wanted to go home, take a hot shower, and climb into bed.

After a few minutes he heard the sound of an unfamiliar motorcycle approaching. Then Frank pulled up on a sleek, fire engine red Italian machine. As Frank tugged off his helmet, Joe walked around the elegant sportbike, whistling.

"Wow, where did you get *this?*" he asked. "And what happened to your bike?"

"It's Ethan DeForrest's personal ride," Frank

answered. "He made me take it instead of mine." He proceeded to fill Joe in on his failed pursuit of Rhino Riordan. "How was your night?" he asked when he'd finished his tale.

"Oh, delightful," Joe responded. "These bikers are some fun." He told Frank about his encounter with Alvie and showed him the nasty slash on his forearm.

"We're a fine pair," Frank said. "I feel like I'm nothing but one big bruise." He thought for a moment. "So what did Copeland have to say about why Alvie had a key to his warehouse?"

"He was puzzled," Joe answered. "He couldn't figure out how Alvie had gotten it."

"I'll bet," Frank said, a sarcastic edge creeping into his voice.

"What's that supposed to mean?" Joe asked, starting to get angry.

"Look, I know he's your pal and all that," Frank said, "but I think it's pretty clear that Copeland is lying. He knows these two bikers, one of them had a key to his warehouse—"

"So, according to you, Lou's behind all this," Joe said. "That's a load of bunk! Lou's the one who put us on to Alvie and Rhino. And what makes you think it isn't DeForrest who's directing them? Man, the guy lends you an exotic sportbike and suddenly he's your hero."

"Okay, let's leave it until tomorrow," Frank said. "We're both tired, sore, and frustrated—

just let it go." He turned away from his younger brother.

"Hey, don't you dismiss me like that. I'm not finished!" Joe exclaimed, grabbing Frank's arm hard.

Frank yanked his arm away, turned back toward Joe, and gave him a powerful shove. "I said, leave it alone," he snarled.

"Don't push me, Frank," Joe snapped. He shoved his brother back even harder. Then all of a sudden his nerves, still jangled from the fight with Alvie, gave out, and he exploded with anger. "I'm tired of you always being the-know-it-all big brother. I've had it with your stubbornness, and it's time someone taught you a lesson." He set his stance, cocked back his fist, and threw a right straight at Frank's jaw.

Chapter 11

FRANK DUCKED under Joe's punch and wrapped his arms around his younger brother's midsection. They grappled furiously, tumbling to the ground in a heap.

Frank and Joe hadn't fought each other like this for years. They rolled around on the ground as if they were little kids again. Frank could feel his own anger rising, but he knew that this fight was silly. "Come on, Joe, cut it out," he shouted, trying to pin down his brother's arms. "This is ridiculous—we're acting like those big jerks Copeland and DeForrest!"

As suddenly as Joe's rage erupted, it disappeared and he stopped struggling. "Okay," he gasped. "You're right." He broke away from Frank and flopped onto his back. They lay on the ground beside the shiny Italian motorcycle, huffing and puffing.

"You okay?" Frank asked when he'd recovered his wind.

"Yeah. You?" Joe replied.

"I guess so," Frank responded.

"What was that all about?" Joe wondered aloud as he sat up.

"Frustration. Exhaustion. It's been a bad night. We just took all our tensions out on each other," Frank said.

"Might as well keep it in the family," Joe joked.

"Yeah, right. Come on, let's go home," Frank said.

They struggled to load Joe's cruiser into the back of the van. Frank said he'd ride the Italian bike home because he didn't want to scratch it. He let out a groan as he swung a leg over its saddle.

"Hey, are you sure you're okay?" Joe asked.

"Nothing some rest won't take care of," Frank answered. "I'll see you at home." He pulled on his helmet, fired up the engine, and roared off. Joe watched him for a second, then climbed into the driver's seat of the van and headed home, ready for a good night's sleep.

* * *

It was almost ten o'clock the next morning when Joe, wrapped in his bathrobe, came shuffling downstairs for breakfast. He found Frank sitting in the living room reading the newspaper, showered, dressed, and seemingly none the worse for wear. Frank glanced up from the paper, muttered, "Morning," and went back to his reading.

"Have you eaten yet?" Joe asked.

Frank folded the paper and put it down. "No, not yet," he answered. "How are you feeling?"

"My arm throbs like crazy, but it doesn't look infected. I poured some antiseptic on it when I came in last night. My shin is purple, but the swelling's gone down—I iced it before I went to bed." He gave his brother a lopsided grin. "I'm a mess, but I'll survive. Yourself?"

"About as well as can be expected for someone who high-sided it at eighty miles an hour, then had a wrestling match with his brother." Frank grinned back at him. "I'm so stiff and sore I feel like someone four times my age. Otherwise, I feel great!"

"Still mad at me?" Joe inquired.

"Yup," Frank responded. "You?"

"Absolutely. My guy isn't the culprit. I think your guy is," Joe said, as he eased himself down onto the couch.

"I've come to exactly the opposite conclusion," Frank said, "and I think you're letting your loyalty blind you. But we still don't have any hard evidence either way. Until we do, this investigation is wide open."

"Agreed," Joe said, nodding. "Let's try not to let our personal feelings get in the way of the truth, whatever it turns out to be." He extended his right hand toward Frank, who reached out and shook it. Frank grimaced as a dull pain gripped his ribs. The doorbell rang just then.

"I'll get it," Joe said, realizing that Frank was really banged up.

"Please do." Frank smiled. Joe heaved himself up off the couch, limped to the front door, and opened it.

It was Lindsey Nichols.

"Hi, Lindsey," Joe said, looking past her to the big bike sitting parked in front of the house. It was a Japanese machine reputed to be the fastest motorcycle money could buy. "Wow," he added, "that's a lot of bike!"

She smiled. "I'm a lot of rider—and don't you forget it."

He held up his hands in mock surrender. "Don't worry, I won't!"

"Actually," she said in a conspiratorial whisper, "I'm here to see Frank. Is he here?"

"Yep," Joe answered. "He'll fill you in on last night."

"Did you have an eventful evening?" she asked.

"Sort of. I'll let Frank tell you about it. I need to run a few errands." They agreed to meet at the motorsports show later that day. Joe led her toward the living room. "Frank, it's Lindsey," he said, and clomped upstairs to shower and dress.

Frank stood as Lindsey entered. "Hi," he said with a self-conscious grin.

"Hi, yourself." She smiled back. "Can I buy you breakfast?"

As Joe stepped out of the shower a few minutes later he heard the dual roar of Lindsey's bike and Frank's borrowed machine departing. Frank had made a remarkable recovery, Joe thought wryly. Lindsey must have been just the right medicine. Almost immediately the phone rang, and he grabbed the extension in his bedroom.

"Hi, Joe, is Frank there?" It was Callie Shaw. Joe rolled his eyes, thankful that he wasn't as popular as his brother these days.

"Uh, no, Callie, he just left. I'm not sure where he went," he said.

For a moment there was silence on the other end of the line, and then Callie said, "He's with Lindsey, isn't he?"

Joe could hear the anger and the hurt in her voice. Now it was his turn to go silent. How could Callie know that, he wondered? She really did have great detective instincts, he thought.

"Uh, I'm not sure," he answered, telling himself that it could be the truth. After all, Frank and Lindsey might have headed off in different directions. . . .

"So do you really think either Copeland or DeForrest is behind all this?" Lindsey Nichols asked Frank Hardy between forkfuls of pancakes. They were seated in a booth at the Bayport Pancake House.

"Maybe not," Frank said. "My brother and I actually fought about it last night. Maybe Alvie and Rhino just hate the idea of new Patriots so much that they're trying to scare off all of you. What bothers me is that there seems to be a connection between Alvie and Copeland."

"The key," Lindsey said.

"That's right," Frank said. "Where did he get it? Anyway, we're still on the case, but we don't have any answers yet."

Lindsey reached across the booth and placed her hand gently on top of Frank's. She squeezed it softly, her luminous green eyes locking with his. "Maybe you should just let it go, Frank," she said. "This is getting too serious—you were almost killed last night."

"Hey, Lindsey, it's okay," Frank reassured her. "Joe and I have been in worse danger for clients we didn't like half as much as we like you."

She smiled, turning away slightly before meeting his gaze again. "That's really what I wanted to talk about," she said. "Look, Frank—how serious are things between you and Callie Shaw?"

Frank was taken aback by such a direct question, and he fumbled for an answer. Finally he said, "Very serious. We've been together for a long time."

"That might be a good reason to try someone new," Lindsey said. "You're the most interesting guy I've met in a long time. I just thought, well, maybe you were ready for a change."

She still hadn't let go of Frank's hand, so now he gently slipped it out from under hers. "Lindsey, I'm really flattered that you think I'm attractive, but I'm really going with Callie."

As Frank spoke, Lindsey's expression darkened and her pretty features quickly formed a scowl. "Come on, Frank, can't you see?" she said, her voice beginning to grow shrill. "We're a perfect match. It's so obvious, not just to us but to everybody else, too. You and Callie don't even have that much in common. She's basically a wimp."

This was a side of Lindsey Frank hadn't seen before. He was surprised by her anger. "Hey, Lindsey, take it easy," he said. Then he spoke more forcefully, "I mean, we hardly know each other. You don't know Callie, and you don't know what we mean to each other. If you want to be my friend you're just going to have to accept that she's my girlfriend, and that isn't going to change."

Lindsey quickly tried to smooth things over. "You're right, Frank, I'm sorry. It's just that I—I really like you. Hey, you can't fault a girl for asking, right?" She offered him a wan smile, then changed the subject. "Anyway, about the case . . ."

Meanwhile, as Frank and Lindsey were finishing breakfast and talking over the case, Joe had driven to Bayport Police Headquarters. Over doughnuts and coffee he filled Officer Con Riley in on events.

"Sounds like you and Frank had a rough night, Joe," Riley said when Joe finished describing their run-ins with Alvie and Rhino. Even though it was still morning, Con already looked rumpled. He continued speaking between bites of a jelly doughnut. "Unfortunately, I don't think you've got enough on these guys to press charges, since there were no witnesses. In fact it could be argued that you provoked them."

"That's right," Joe said. "The only witnesses were the other Sinners, and they thought we were trying to steal their motorcycles. But I didn't come here to press charges. Right now I'd just like to know what you have on these guys."

Riley shrugged. "Not much. They've lived in or around Bayport all their lives. They're both habitual, minor criminals. Both have twenty-year records for petty theft, trafficking in stolen goods, assault. . . . Rhino still doesn't have any visible means of support. At least Alvie has a trade."

"What's that?" Joe asked.

"He owns his own locksmith shop," Riley answered.

Joe mulled over the case with Con Riley for a few more minutes, then left the station and drove straight over to the motorsports show at the Bayport Fairgrounds. He parked beside Lindsey and Frank's bikes, glad to see they were already there. He was eager to tell his brother that Alvie Moore was a locksmith, which meant that he could have copied the key to Copeland's warehouse without Copeland's knowledge. A skilled locksmith knows how to make a wax model from a lock, and then copy the key from the model.

As Joe approached the adjacent Patriot booths he heard loud voices and guessed that DeForrest and Copeland were feuding again. He hurried over, ignoring the pain in his knee as he jogged.

"Put up or shut up!" Copeland yelled at his rival, as Del Nichols stood between them, urging calm. "I'm tired of going around and around with this!" He turned angrily toward Del Nichols. "Look, if we leave this to the courts it's going to take years before this ownership issue is decided. So I'm willing to lay it all on the line, winner take all."

"What are you talking about, Lou?" DeForrest asked.

"You want to know which of us has the better bike, right?" Copeland asked Nichols, who nodded in agreement.

"Fine," Copeland continued. He turned back to DeForrest. "My bike against your bike. A race, and winner takes all. Can you handle that?"

"Any time, any place!" DeForrest snarled. "My Commander will blow that piddly little Minuteman off the road. What do *you* say, Del?"

Del Nichols said, "Sounds good to me, boys. Let's do it tomorrow. We'll start from here and make a thirty-mile course. Make a show of it. We'll get the press here, hype it up for publicity. Fair enough?"

"Done!" DeForrest said.

"Done!" Copeland agreed.

"So who's going to ride the bikes? You two?" Del Nichols chuckled, rolling his eyes at the two portly, middle-aged men.

"No way," Copeland said. "I'm putting the best person I can find on my bike." He looked around as if he might pick someone out of the crowd. His eyes fixed on Joe. "There's my rider," he said, pointing. "Joe Hardy."

Joe started to hold up his hands to protest, but just then Frank and Lindsey ambled onto the scene together, deep in conversation.

"Oh yeah?" DeForrest quickly countered. "Then there's *my* rider!

Chapter 12

DEFORREST WAS POINTING straight at Frank.

"Rider for what?" a baffled Frank asked. Joe quickly filled Frank and Lindsey in on what Copeland, DeForrest, and Nichols had in mind, then added, "I don't think it's a great idea, myself. That is, not unless we all come clean to Ethan and Lou." He looked meaningfully from Lindsey to Del Nichols.

"Hey, at this point it's okay with me." Del Nichols shrugged.

"What are you people talking about?" Copeland asked.

"We've been working for Del and Lindsey. They asked us to help assess your companies," Frank explained.

"You what?" DeForrest burst out.

"You've been spying on us! How dare you," Copeland said, turning toward Del Nichols angrily.

"Hey, you two were acting so all-fired secretive I had to do something to get information," Del answered. "You're both so paranoid you're not acting like businessmen anymore! I can't get a demo ride out of either of you, and you're both asking me to put up big bucks to back you. If I didn't believe a new company could be successful, I'd have bailed out a long time ago 'cause you guys have both been holding out on me." He and the two Patriot builders glowered at one another.

Lindsey's eyes glowed with excitement. "That's telling them, Dad!" she exclaimed. She turned on Copeland and DeForrest with an edge in her voice. "If we left things up to you two you'd waste all your time squabbling and there'd never be any new Patriots!" she said. "Now we have a way to settle this whole thing without dragging it through the courts forever. So why don't you stop arguing and start working out the details of this race."

If she thought her vehemence would calm them down she was mistaken. Both men turned toward her angrily, and Copeland snarled, "Del, your young lady here is getting too big for her britches."

"Yeah, Lindsey," DeForrest added. "You've got a lot of nerve telling us what to do! Why don't you leave it to the grown-ups to work this out?"

"Maybe I would," she said harshly, "if I saw any grown-ups around here! Come on, Dad," she said. "Let's just cut these two losers loose—trying to deal with them just isn't worth the grief."

"She's got a point," Del said. "This is just getting to be too much trouble."

"Okay, okay, everybody calm down," Frank said. Suddenly he imagined this turning into another brawl. He cast a glance at Lindsey. It seemed to him that she was overreacting, that her comments were just fanning the flames instead of cooling them down. Frank noticed that a heated exchange had started between Del Nichols and his daughter. He couldn't hear their whispers, but he noticed that Joe was eavesdropping and made a mental note to ask him what they said later.

Once Frank was sure he had everyone's attention, he continued. "For the moment, let's assume that neither of you is trying to kill the other or destroy the other's bike," he said to Copeland and DeForrest. "And let's assume those two one-percenters are responsible. Or at least that they're the likely suspects—"

"And that they'll get caught before they do

any real harm," interrupted Lindsey, who seemed to have regained her composure. "In which case, we're back where we started, trying to decide which Patriot to support. I think this race is a great idea, and it's a fair way to help my dad decide between the two bikes." She turned with a smile toward Frank, who could sense she was making an effort to appear reasonable. "I've raced against you two, and I know you're evenly matched. What do you say, guys?"

Joe wasn't the least bit surprised when Frank answered, "I'm game. What about you, Joe?"

When Joe hesitated, Copeland gave him a beseeching glance.

"Well, I'm eager to test the Minuteman," Joe said. "And I do think we can blow the Commander away, so let's do it!"

"Then it's set," DeForrest said. "Come on, Frank, let's schedule you some practice time this afternoon," he said, throwing a big arm around Frank's shoulders.

Joe and Copeland made similar arrangements, and then Joe took Frank aside for a moment. "I want another shot at Alvie Moore," he told his brother, "and I just happen to have the address of his locksmith shop."

"Let's go check it out," Frank said. "By the way, Joe, I noticed you were listening to that little exchange between Lindsey and Del while

I was trying to calm our friends down. Did you happen to hear what they said?"

"As a matter of fact, I did," Joe said. "Lindsey said Del was finally paying attention to what she had to say and Del said, 'Maybe that's because you're finally saying some things worth listening to.' "

"Hmm," Frank said, thinking that maybe he was beginning to glimpse a new side of Lindsey.

"You're pretty quiet," Joe said to Frank as he pulled their black van out of the fairgrounds parking lot a little later. The others were going to work out the details of the race, and they'd promised to brief the Hardys later that afternoon. "Something on your mind?" he asked. Frank stared into space, a slight frown on his face, and didn't respond. Joe said, "Let me guess. Could it be Lindsey Nichols?"

"Not too hard to figure that one out, was it?" Frank said with a tight smile.

"Callie called just after you left the house," Joe said. "Maybe you should have a talk with Callie," he suggested. "We can stop by her house on the way—Alvie can wait."

"That might not be a bad idea," Frank said.

"Hi, guys, this is a pleasant surprise," Callie Shaw greeted the Hardys at her front door. "I didn't expect to see much of you until this case was solved. *Is* it solved?"

"Hardly," Frank answered. "I just wanted to stop by to say hello."

"Well, then, I'm going to hold you to your promise of keeping me informed," Callie said. "I want to know everything that's happened to you two since I saw you yesterday."

"We've been pretty busy, and I'm pretty hungry," Joe said. "Frank, why don't you tell her about it, and if you don't mind I'll see if Mrs. Shaw has anything interesting in the fridge."

Once he and Callie were comfortably seated on the couch, Frank began with the threatening note to Del Nichols. He explained how they'd learned the identities of the two bikers, then described their confrontation with the biker gang.

"That wasn't the worst of it," Joe added, returning from the kitchen with a plate of fried chicken and potato salad that Mrs. Shaw had fixed for him. "Those two goons almost killed us!"

Frank shot Joe a hard glance that told him he didn't want to play this up for fear of alarming Callie. It was too late.

"This is really getting out of hand," Callie said. "Why don't you just leave it to the police."

"We're already too involved," Frank said.

"So what happened with those two bikers?" Callie asked.

There was no way for Frank to avoid the seriousness of their run-ins with Alvie and Rhino, but he tried to recount them in a matter-of-fact tone.

"And what do you mean you're already too involved?" Callie asked. Frank told her about their commitment to race the untried motorcycles the next day. She rolled her eyes and let out a little whistle. She thought for a moment, then asked, "Have you really discounted Copeland and DeForrest as suspects?"

"Well, you never completely discount anybody," Joe said, "but they seem less and less likely."

"You've told me over and over again not to ignore any of the possibilities, right?" Callie asked. The brothers agreed. "Then what about Del and Lindsey Nichols?"

"I don't see what motive they'd have," Frank said. "Del wants to revive the Patriot. Lindsey wants to please her father. Why would they want to harm the companies they want to acquire?" He paused. "Unless, of course, DeForrest and Copeland were put under a lot of pressure, then they'd be forced to sell out more cheaply." He wrinkled his brow. "I guess that's possible."

Callie admitted that it was a long shot.

"The bikers really seem like the ones," Joe said. "Now we just have to prove it."

"Well, I want to be at that race tomorrow," Callie said. "And I'm sure Vanessa will want to be there, too."

"As long as you're both rooting for *me,*" Joe said, giving Callie a wink. "Listen," he said to Frank, "we'd better be going if we want to check out Alvie Moore."

"Why don't you give us a minute, Joe?" Frank said.

Joe waved goodbye to Callie, stopped off in the kitchen to throw away the chicken bones and put his dirty plate in the dishwasher, then went out to wait for his brother by the van.

"What's the matter, Frank?" Callie asked.

"I'm really sorry that this case has caused problems between us. I really don't want to hurt you."

"I know that, silly." Callie smiled as she walked him to the door. "I'll see you tomorrow at the race," she said.

"I'll be looking for you," Frank answered, and jogged over to the van.

"You look better already," Joe said.

"Yeah—it'll work out," Frank said.

"So let's go. We've got a little weasel to catch," Joe said, and they piled into the van and drove off.

* * *

Frank and Joe were parked at the curb in front of a small bungalow in a very seedy neighborhood. "That's the place," Joe said.

"Doesn't look like much, does it?" Frank answered. Unsupervised children played in front of several ramshackle houses on the block, while a small group of teenage toughs loitered in front of a convenience store across the street. Next to a bungalow was a plumbing supply store, and the bungalow itself had a faded sign out front that said Locksmith.

"I'm guessing Alvie lives here, too," Joe said. "Come on—let's pay him a visit."

They walked to the front door. It was locked, and a sign in the window read Closed—Please Come Again.

"That's odd," Frank noted. "I'd expect the shop to be open in the middle of a Saturday afternoon." They peered in the window and could see that the front room was set up as the shop, with a counter, a small cash register, and Alvie's locksmithing equipment.

"Why don't we try the side door?" Joe asked. "That's probably the entrance to the living quarters." They cautiously followed the narrow driveway to the side door. Joe was about to climb the three steps to the door when Frank stopped him.

"Look," Frank said, pointing toward the back of the house. Alvie's Patriot was parked in the paved-over backyard, chained to a metal grommet buried in the cement. Parked beside the bike was a small pickup truck with "Alvie Moore Locksmith" painted on the door.

"Looks like he's home," Joe said.

They approached the door again. There was a large window next to the door, but its curtain was drawn. Joe noticed that one pane of the window glass was shattered. There was a hole in the curtain, about a half inch in diameter, behind the shattered pane.

"What do you make of that?" Joe asked his brother, pointing to the broken pane.

"Why don't we ask Alvie?" Frank suggested. He knocked on the door.

"Hello? Anyone home?" Frank called. There was no answer. Frank hesitantly pushed on the door handle. The door opened into a grimy kitchen. The sink was full of dirty dishes. There were crumbs and wrappers all over the counters. Joe, who was behind Frank, whispered, "Do you think he's home?"

"He sure is," Frank answered flatly as he stared into the gloom of the little kitchen. Then Joe saw what Frank was gaping at.

Directly in line with the shattered windowpane, sprawled on the floor of the kitchen, lay Alvie Moore, facedown in a pool of blood.

Chapter 13

"IS HE DEAD?" Joe asked.

Frank knelt by the body and gingerly felt the neck for a pulse. "Very," he said. Frank could feel that the body was quite cold, indicating that Alvie had been dead for hours. The blood on the floor around his head was already mostly congealed. Frank felt a wave of nausea. He'd seen a number of corpses, but he was hardly used to stumbling upon a gory scene like this. He hoped he never would be.

"Careful—don't disturb anything," Joe said.

"Thanks for the advice," Frank answered. They hunched over the dead biker together, and Joe pointed to a mass of matted hair just over

Alvie's left ear. They could make out a small hole in the man's temple.

"Small caliber gun," Joe said. "I know this guy tried to kill me last night, but still—"

Frank could see that his brother was as upset as he was, but they were both making every effort not to let it get to them. Their dad always told them how important it was for a detective to remain detached, especially at the scene of a crime. Frank pointed to a single lamp in the room. It was on, and although it didn't cast much light in the middle of the afternoon, it must have illuminated the whole room at night.

"He would have been silhouetted against the window curtain," Frank speculated. "That explains the broken window and the hole in the curtain."

"Someone's a pretty good shot," Joe said. They rose and walked over to the window. Frank used a pen from his pocket to draw back the curtain a bit so that they could see their van parked at the curb.

"It's a straight shot," Frank pointed out. "Just about twenty-five yards."

"A small-bore handgun isn't accurate at that kind of range," Joe added. "It had to be some kind of a rifle."

"So the killer sat at the curb last night after Alvie came home," Frank said, reconstructing the crime. "He waited until Alvie was outlined against the curtain. He squeezed off one shot, then took off."

"I wonder if the killer was on a bike," Joe said.

"Are you thinking that maybe Rhino decided to dissolve the partnership?" Frank asked.

"That's one possibility," Joe said. "But right now I'm thinking that we'd better call the cops."

"This is exactly the way you found him, you didn't move anything?" Con Riley asked, after surveying the scene.

"Come on, Con, what do you think we are," Joe said, "a couple of amateurs?"

"Just asking," the officer said. He had arrived several minutes earlier with a homicide team, and now his fellow officers were carefully examining the crime scene for clues.

"Judging from the accuracy of the shot and the small entry wound, I'd guess it was a twenty-two, Con," Joe said. "Just like the gun that was used to shoot at me and Lou Copeland the other night."

"Which doesn't necessarily mean it was the *same* gun," Riley pointed out.

Joe said, "Just a coincidence, right?"

"I'm considering the possibilities, that's all," Riley answered. "Try this scenario—from what you've told me, Alvie here and his big buddy, Rhino, were real fanatics for Patriot bikes. They were ticked off about the plans to build new ones. So they were probably the ones trying to scare off Copeland, DeForrest, and the Nicholses. If these two bikers had a falling out, Rhino might have decided it was too risky to have his partner-in-crime running around out there. So he decided to eliminate the risk."

"We thought of that one," Frank said. "So now what happens?"

"Now I put out an all-points bulletin for Rhino so we can pick him up. If he didn't kill Alvie, he might have a pretty good idea who did," Riley said. "You two take off and let us do our job here. I'll keep you posted about what we find. I trust you'll do the same for me?"

The Hardys agreed and returned to their van. As they drove off, Joe asked Frank, "Do you really think that Rhino killed Alvie? I sure don't."

"I hear you, Joe," Frank said. "It doesn't make sense. What motive would he have for killing his best riding buddy? And if he did kill him, why bother to wait outside and ambush Alvie instead of just knocking and getting him to let him in?"

"Not much point in risking being seen if you don't have to," Joe said. "A twenty-two doesn't make much noise, but why take the chance? Besides, I just don't see a huge guy like Rhino using a twenty-two. It would be like a toy to him. A macho guy like that would have something bigger. So what do you think—do we try to find Rhino?"

"We already have a couple of motorcycles waiting for us. The race is in less than twenty-four hours. Why don't we leave Rhino to the cops?"

"Makes sense to me," Joe said. "But we'd better warn everybody. Whoever the culprit is has killed once in cold blood. The first time's always the hardest. It gets easier after that, so I don't think he'll hesitate to kill again."

Later that afternoon Joe Hardy was flying past fields and farms on the outskirts of Bayport. The backcountry two-lane roads were the perfect place to test a motorcycle, and Joe was really wringing out Lou Copeland's Minuteman. In fact, he was following the thirty-mile route that Copeland, DeForrest, and Nichols had mapped out for the race. The Hardys were familiar with these roads but not necessarily at high speeds.

Joe was very impressed with the Minuteman's performance. It was smooth, light, nimble, and quick. It delivered strong, even power with good acceleration throughout the rev range.

It would never be a threat to sports machines like the Italian bike DeForrest had loaned

Frank, but it wasn't meant to be. That Italian machine was basically a racer with headlights tacked on to make it legal. Those bikes bent their riders into pretzel-like crouches and had suspensions so stiff that every imperfection in the road hit like a sledgehammer.

In contrast, the Minuteman was a beautifully balanced package. It had plenty of speed and excellent handling, and was comfortable enough to spend a whole day in the saddle with a passenger on the back.

When he finally returned to Lou Copeland's shop after spending nearly two hours on the Minuteman, Joe was wearing a wide grin.

"What do you think?" Copeland asked.

"Wow," Joe said. "That is one sweet set of wheels."

"Any complaints?" Copeland asked.

"Yeah—that I don't own one," Joe said. "Really, Lou, you got it exactly right. It has all the character of the classic British bikes like Nortons and Triumphs, but it feels completely modern. And it might be the best-looking bike I've ever seen."

"Now we've just got to hope that it can beat DeForrest's monster," Copeland said. "I'm sure he's built a good bike."

"Sounds like you still have a little respect for him," Joe said.

"Of course I do," Copeland responded. "You

saw his prototype—he really sweated the details to get that Commander look. That bike is an instant classic."

"So's this one," Joe told him, patting the crimson gas tank of the Minuteman. "I can't imagine that the original Patriots were anywhere as good as this."

"They weren't," Copeland said. "That is, with the exception of the Lightning."

"Never heard of it," Joe said.

"I'm not surprised. They only built a handful of them in the early sixties. It was a last gasp for the factory—but it was a good one. The Patriot Lightning was the best bike of its time, and no one matched it for nearly ten years. But it was just too little, too late to save the company." Copeland wore a wistful expression.

"What were the Lightnings like?" Joe asked.

"They only came in black," Copeland told him, "with a chrome lightning bolt on the side of the gas tank. Lean, mean machines, based on the last Minuteman model. But they revved much higher. They put out almost seventy horsepower—which was a phenomenal number in those days. For racing, a good mechanic could get another ten horsepower out of one."

"Wait a second," Joe said. "These Lightnings revved *higher* than standard Patriots?"

"That's right," Copeland said.

"But otherwise they sounded a lot like them?" Joe continued.

"Right," Copeland said. "Why do you ask?"

"Because that's just the difference between the bike the mystery rider was on and all the other Patriots I've heard, including the Minuteman," Joe said, tapping the tank of Copeland's new bike. "It was winding out higher, really screaming."

Copeland tried to remember. "You know, that bike we heard after we were shot at—it could have been a Lightning. It's been almost twenty years since I heard one, though."

While his friend was pondering that old sound, Joe was remembering a picture he'd seen just the day before. A picture in a frame.

"Lou," he asked, "did any Lightnings ever make it to the Bayport area?"

"Just one as far as I know," Lou Copeland answered. "I remember seeing it on display in DeForrest's showroom for almost six months before it sold. But it was too much bike for the guy who bought it, and it kept changing hands. It finally got rebuilt as a racer, nearly ten years after it came out of the factory. And even then it was the hottest thing around. That old bike used to blow away the newest, fastest bikes in the area." He smiled at the recollection. "Fact is, I lost against that bike more than once. Of course, a big part of that was the Lightning's rider."

Joe asked the next question, knowing what the answer would be but hoping that he was wrong. "And who was that rider, Lou?"

"It was Del Nichols, Joe."

Chapter 14

JOE HAD A HARD TIME hiding his excitement. He was convinced that this was the first solid lead in the case since they'd figured out the identities of the two bikers. Measuring his words carefully, he asked, "Do you have any idea whatever became of Del Nichols's Lightning?"

Copeland shrugged his shoulders. "Who knows?" he responded. "Maybe he sold it. Or he might even still have it tucked under a tarp somewhere. He owns a few warehouses and garages around town besides the dealership. But you know, I don't think of old Del as the sentimental type. For all I know, he might have sent it to the junk heap years ago." He paused, then asked, "You think the mystery rider is using Del's old bike?"

"I think I should definitely try to find out what became of it," Joe said.

Meanwhile, in Lakedale, Frank was testing the Commander on a closed racecourse, the Lakedale Raceway. It was a stockcar loop, but the owner was a friend of Ethan DeForrest and had given them a few hours of practice time. DeForrest had also given Frank a map of the actual racecourse, and Frank planned to check it out on the Italian sportbike on his way home. For now, he was more concerned with the Commander, and he was pleased with what he was finding.

The thing that impressed Frank most about the big bike was its torque—how hard its engine pulled on the low end of its powerband. He didn't think he'd ever been on a bike that roared out of a turn with such authority, not even the Italian street racer Ethan had loaned him. The bike felt as solid as an anvil all the way up to its top speed of a hundred and twenty miles an hour. He hoped that would be enough in tomorrow's race, but he suspected that the lighter Minuteman was faster at the top. He was also concerned about the Commander's handling. It was excellent for such a large machine, but again, the Minuteman was almost sure to be more nimble.

After several strong all-out practice laps, Frank rolled to a stop at the finish line where Ethan DeForrest waited eagerly.

"Nice, isn't it?" DeForrest asked.

"Absolutely. It's a great road bike, but—" Frank hesitated.

"But what?" DeForrest said.

"That's the problem," Frank said. "It's a big, plush road bike. I wouldn't hesitate to ride this bike all the way to California with a full pack of luggage and gear. But it might be out of its element in a race."

"I've thought about that," DeForrest said. "That's why we picked out thirty miles of back roads instead of holding the race at a track. It should even out whatever advantage either machine has. Some spots will favor the Commander's torque, others the Minuteman's nimbleness. The determining factor is really going to be which Hardy is the better rider." He paused, then offered some more coaching. "I don't think you're going to find the top end tomorrow—the straightaways we picked aren't long enough. Meanwhile, the turns aren't so tight that you won't be able to push this big old thing real hard." He slapped Frank's shoulder. "You'll do fine, and so will the Commander."

"I'll try not to disappoint you," Frank said.

"But you know, I keep thinking that it's too bad you and Copeland are at such loggerheads. You've each got great bikes. It's a shame you can't work together."

"I've felt the same way more than once since this whole thing began," DeForrest said. "But it's gone too far now to get back together again—and I guess I'm at least half to blame for that."

"If you're willing to admit that, then maybe you two aren't as far apart as you think," Frank suggested.

"I wish I could share your optimism, Frank," DeForrest said with a smile and a shake of his head "Come on, why don't you take another circuit around the track? I want you to know this bike inside out by tomorrow."

It was almost closing time when Joe Hardy showed up at the Bayport showroom of Nichols Motorsports. He was greeted by a salesperson who said he'd go find Del or Lindsey for him. Within a few minutes, Lindsey came out from the office area, walking briskly toward him across the showroom floor.

"Hi, Joe." She smiled brightly when she saw who was waiting for her. "I'm surprised to see you here. I thought you'd be out practicing on the Minuteman."

"Well, I spent a couple of hours on it," he

said, "but then I just got this overwhelming urge to buy one of these." He pointed out an immense full-rig touring bike, virtually a two-wheeled car, loaded with hard saddlebags and trunk, a huge windscreen, and an elaborate stereo system. Such bikes were enormously expensive, and their typical riders were couples in their fifties. Lindsey gave him a puzzled look.

"Excuse me?" she said.

"Just joking," he said, giving her a big grin. "That's not exactly my style."

"I didn't think so," she said, "but you Hardys are full of surprises. So what really brings you here?"

"I was wondering if I could talk to your father," he asked.

"Dad's not here," Lindsey said. "I think he's in town making arrangements for the race tomorrow, which is becoming a big deal. Maybe I can help. What's up?"

"Maybe you can," Joe said. "You've only been here a few weeks, but you seem to be on top of everything."

"I think my dad has finally realized that I'm the only kid he's got," she said. "If he's going to pass all this down to anyone, I'm it. So he's been teaching me all about the business. For years it seemed like he didn't even know I existed, no matter how hard I tried to please him. But now we're getting along."

"It's hard to imagine anyone ignoring you," Joe said, flirting a bit.

"Why, thank you, Joe," Lindsey said, batting her eyelids at him exaggeratedly. "But if that was a come-on, forget it. I'm having enough trouble with *one* Hardy."

Joe knew Lindsey wasn't taking his flirting any more seriously than he'd meant it. But he felt a wave of sympathy for her as he said, "You know, I wish Frank wasn't a problem for you—or you for him."

"He really seems to like Callie," Lindsey said, biting her lower lip.

"He does," Joe agreed.

"But there's a spark between me and Frank, too," Lindsey said.

"I've noticed," Joe said. "That happens sometimes, but when you're already involved with someone else, you've just got to get over it."

"Well," Lindsey said, "Frank's pretty special."

Joe tried to read Lindsey's expression but couldn't. He decided she was quite a bit deeper than she seemed at first. There seemed to be some sort of sadness lurking beneath her gung-ho attitude and cheerful grin. "There are a lot of nice guys at Bayport High who don't have girlfriends," Joe said. "I could introduce you to some of them if you like."

"That might not be a bad idea," she agreed, brightening. "But you didn't come here to talk about my social life, did you? So what was it? Come on, talk!"

"Actually, it's just that I'm an incorrigible bike lover, and Lou Copeland mentioned something that I just had to check out." He told her about the Lightning. "I really wanted to find out if it still existed."

"Hey, I remember that bike!" Lindsey said. "It was a beauty. Come on, I'll show it to you, it's way in the back of the warehouse."

She led the way through the shop, past the parts and accessories departments, past the mechanics in the back, and deep into the warehouse. Way in back, behind the new stock, were a bunch of battered old bikes—enough to fill a junkyard, it seemed to Joe. Against a wall in a dingy corner was a bike under a canvas tarp.

"I think that's it," Lindsey said. Joe was eager to see it. He was half-convinced that this was the bike he'd heard, and that Del Nichols was the mystery rider. On the other hand, it was so crowded back there that he wondered whether it could have been squeezed out past the other machines. What about that thick layer of dust caked on the Lightning's tarp, too?

Lindsey pulled the cover back, revealing the old racer.

It was a mess, a testimony to years of neglect. The bike was covered with cobwebs; its paint and chrome were faded, pitted with rust. Its tires were cracked and rotting. Joe could see that it hadn't been moved in years. Masking his disappointment, Joe took a few minutes to examine the old bike while Lindsey pointed out the features that had made it such a terror on the racetrack.

"I wish I could have seen it in its prime," Joe said.

"Yeah, me, too," Lindsey agreed. They made their way back through the dealership, stopping at last in front of Del Nichols's office.

"Well, I guess I'm going to head home," Joe told Lindsey.

"Yeah, I've got a lot to do," she said. "Dad's been having me close up on evenings when he can't get back here." She had a thought. "Say, maybe we can make that old Lightning a winter project. I'll bet we could have it running like new by springtime."

"Wouldn't that be something," Joe said, imagining how much fun it could be to restore the bike using all of Nichols Motorsports' terrific resources.

He turned to leave, passing the trophy case, and paused. A thought just occurred to him. "Hey, Lindsey, is this the Lightning in this old photograph?" he asked, pointing out the picture that had caught his eye the last time he was there.

She joined him at the case. "Can't see too

much of the bike, but it sure looks like it," she said, squinting at the photo.

Joe pointed to Del and the pit crew. "Don't they look happy!" he said. "Who were those guys, anyway?"

"Hmm—this looks like Mike Anderson. He still works for Dad, managing a dealership. As for the others, I don't know. I wasn't born when the picture was taken."

Joe thought there was something very familiar about the two pit crew members in front. He decided to keep his suspicion to himself. The guys in the picture were very young, very clean-cut, but Joe could plainly see that one was small and wiry, while the other was a big, bulky brute. If you aged them twenty years, added long, stringy hair and scruffy beards, dressed them up in biker colors . . .

Joe was starting to think that Del Nichols knew Alvie Moore and Rhino Riordan very well—as members of his pit crew back when he was racing the Patriot Lightning!

Chapter 15

It was nearly ten o'clock when Frank and Joe finally found themselves back home and at the kitchen table. As they built elaborate sandwiches out of the stock of cold cuts, cheeses, pickles, and other fillings left for them in the refrigerator, they quizzed each other.

"How was DeForrest's bike?" Joe asked.

"Oh, pretty good" was Frank's noncommittal answer. "How was Copeland's?"

"Okay, I guess," Joe responded. He tried to suppress a grin but couldn't. "Who am I fooling? The Minuteman is terrific. It's a blast to ride!"

Now Frank let down his reserve, too, and

said, "So's the Commander. It's a great bike! Let me tell you about my practice session."

They regaled each other with stories about the Commander and the Minuteman. After listening to each other's performance assessments, they agreed that the two bikes were very different types of machines.

"This race is going to be like comparing apples and bananas," Frank said. "There's nothing wrong with either of them, they're just designed for different purposes. And neither one is a racing machine. It's really a shame they can't both be produced."

"Imagine a complete, modern Patriot line," Joe said. "The Commander, the Minuteman, something a bit smaller for beginners, and brand-new Lightnings."

"I wonder if that's occurred to Del Nichols," Frank said, then stopped abruptly. "Wait a second. What's a Lightning?"

Joe filled his brother in, and Frank was all ears, especially when Joe told him about seeing Del Nichols's old Lightning at the dealership.

"But you say it was a wreck," he said.

"That's right," Joe said. "But I'm really starting to think that Callie's hunch was right, that everything leads back to Del Nichols somehow." He told Frank about the photograph, and the two very young men from Del's pit crew. "I'm sure it's Alvie and Rhino in that picture."

Frank mulled this over. "Here's another point about Del," he said. "Remember that almost the first thing Lindsey told us about him is that he's an expert shot with a rifle. He could easily have made the shot from the curb that killed Alvie and the one that blew out Lou Copeland's windshield."

"The question is, why would he go this far to sabotage projects he wants to back financially?" Joe said. "It doesn't make sense."

"And how do Alvie and Rhino fit in?" Frank said. But their analysis was cut short by a loud knock on the door. "I'll get it," Frank said.

As Frank headed for the door, Joe noticed that his older brother was still moving stiffly. Joe wasn't surprised, since he didn't feel one hundred percent yet, either.

Frank returned, followed by Con Riley.

"Hey, Con—we weren't expecting you tonight," Joe said as he stood to shake hands with the police officer. "What's up?"

"We found your buddy, Rhino Riordan," Riley told them.

"Hey, that's great," Frank said with enthusiasm. "Is he talking?"

"Well, not exactly," Riley said. "He's in Lakedale Hospital in a deep coma."

"What happened?" Joe wanted to know.

"We're not sure," Riley said. "The Highway Patrol found him and his bike in a ditch along the road out toward Lakedale. He must have gone down shortly after forcing you off the road, Frank. He hit his head on a rock by the roadside, and that little beanie helmet he was wearing didn't do much to protect him."

"It's hard to believe he could have an accident like that, Con," Frank argued. "The guy's an expert rider."

"Did I say it was an accident?" Riley asked. "We dug this out of his front tire." He reached into his pocket, pulled out a plastic bag containing a little lump of lead, and dropped it on the kitchen table. The Hardys stared at it.

"A twenty-two round," Joe said.

"It matches the bullet we found on Lou Copeland's front seat and the one that killed Alvie Moore," Con told them. "Somebody's a *very* good shot."

"We have an idea who that might be," Frank said. The brothers shared their suspicions about Del Nichols.

"If you guys are right, then you could be in danger tomorrow during the race," Riley said. "I think I'd better be out at the fairgrounds with a few of Bayport's finest. We'll keep a close eye on Nichols, but I want you two to promise me you'll be careful while you're chasing each other all over the back roads."

* * *

On Sunday morning Frank and Joe drove their van to the Bayport Fairgrounds. Loaded in the back were two complete sets of racing leathers, including boots, gloves, and top-quality helmets. The weather was cool, clear, and calm—perfect for racing.

As the Hardys parked their van, they noticed a sizeable crowd had already gathered. They climbed out of the van and started working their way through the crowd, spotting many of their friends and schoolmates.

Biff Hooper grabbed Joe's sleeve as they passed him and joked, "How'd you guys luck into this?"

"Clean living," Joe quipped, smiling at his big buddy.

"So which one of you is favored to win?" asked Tony Prito, who was with Biff.

"I am," both brothers said in unison. They faced each other in mock anger, then chuckled as they made their way to the two Patriot booths, where Ethan DeForrest, Lou Copeland, and Del and Lindsey Nichols were waiting.

"Hey, Joe, ready to rumble?" Lou greeted his rider. "Let's show them how a real motorcycle runs."

"We're going to make you eat those words. Right, Frank?" DeForrest boomed. Both men seemed in surprisingly good humor considering the stakes. Frank realized that this must be a relief to them. Racing was something they both understood, and the conflict between them would finally be decided, rather than dragging on forever in the courts. He wished he could feel as enthusiastic, but that wasn't likely since both he and Joe knew that the stakes were even higher than Copeland and DeForrest realized.

Frank and Joe each huddled for last-minute instructions. They were reassured to find out that both Copeland and DeForrest had driven the route earlier to make sure it was clear of any nasty surprises, like slippery sand or oil spills.

Frank noted the extra police presence under the direction of Officer Con Riley, who he knew would be paying special attention to Del Nichols. It would be very difficult for Del to slip away if he was the mystery biker. Once they had received their final briefings, Frank and Joe got together and wished each other luck.

"Hey, guys, remember us?" Vanessa Bender called in a lilting voice behind them. The Hardys turned to see Callie and Vanessa approaching.

"I'm glad to see you," Frank said to Callie.

"I wish I could say the same about your new best pal," Callie answered, shooting a glance toward Lindsey Nichols. Lindsey was peering at them expressionless from behind a pair of dark sunglasses.

"Can you give me a minute?" he asked Callie. "I'm going to get this straightened out once and for all, okay?"

"Be my guest," she answered.

"Hey, Lindsey, got a second?" he called.

"Sure, what's on your mind?" she answered coolly.

"I think you know," he answered.

"Well, it's pretty obvious you've made your choice." She nodded at Callie.

"Look, I hope there's no bad feelings about this. I really do like you—"

"But only as a friend, right Frank?" Lindsey interrupted, and Frank was surprised by the edge to her voice.

"I'm sorry if you're hurt—" he said.

"Don't flatter yourself," she snapped. Then she seemed to think better of her reaction. "Sorry, Frank, that was uncalled for." She stuck out her hand. "Friends?"

"You bet," he said, and they shook hands.

"All right, then—why don't you go out there and win a race," Lindsey said. She gave Frank a quick clap on the back, then went off to join her father. Now it was Del Nichols's turn to glare at Frank, who simply returned the glare and made no attempt to hide his suspicions.

"Everything okay?" Callie asked when Frank returned to the Patriot booths.

"Yeah, sure, no problem," Frank responded. "She just needed to simmer down. Come on, let's get this race on," Frank shouted over to Joe, Copeland, and DeForrest.

Soon Joe and Frank were squared off, side by side on the new Patriots, at the entrance to the fairgrounds parking lot. They revved their engines, and the crowd gathered behind them. Del Nichols stood in front of them with a starter pistol in hand. Copeland and DeForrest shouted last-minute instructions to the brothers, which neither of them could hear over the roaring of their engines.

Joe smiled at Vanessa. Frank gave Callie a reassuring wink. He looked around for Lindsey, but couldn't spot her in the crowd. She must be behind him somewhere, he guessed, as he flipped down his visor.

When Nichols fired his starter pistol into the air, the report was loud enough to be heard over the roar of the big engines. The Hardys nailed the throttles of their bikes, and the two brand-new Patriots leapt forward. The race was on.

For the first ten or twelve minutes they hurtled down the road side by side, with no more than a bike length between them. Their competitive juices were flowing, and there was no doubt that each brother was trying his best to win the race.

Joe's Minuteman was definitely more nimble, and he gained ground on the turns. Coming out of the turns, though, the huge torque of the

Commander enabled Frank to reel him in, and they ran neck and neck to the next turn, where they'd repeat the sequence. They were averaging well over seventy miles an hour over country lanes. At this rate it would take them just over twenty minutes to cover the thirty-mile course.

Almost fifteen minutes into the race, Frank spotted something in his rearview mirror. It was a black dot that quickly grew into a dark figure on a motorcycle. He used his tongue to click on the bike-to-bike communicator that he and Joe had installed in their helmets.

"Can you read me?" he asked.

"Loud and clear," Joe's voice answered in his ear.

"That's good, 'cause we've got company. Check behind us."

Joe dared a quick glance over his shoulder. The mystery rider was coming up fast behind them. He had his right hand on the throttle of his bike. His left hand held a long, slim rifle, and Joe watched as he took aim at them!

Chapter 16

"WE'VE GOTTA WEAVE, JOE," Joe heard Frank's voice crackle over the intercom.

"On your signal, Frank," Joe said. "Make it quick. He's about to open fire."

"Ready—*now!*" Frank barked.

Together they cranked back on the throttles of their bikes, downshifting at the same time for increased acceleration. The two new Patriots shot forward. The needles of their speedometers swept up over the hundred mile an hour mark and the wind whistled past their helmets.

Now they began to weave back and forth across the road, changing lanes and exchanging leads. They hoped that their deadly dance would make it impossible for their pursuer to draw a bead on either of them. They knew it was a wildly dangerous maneuver that required split-second timing to avoid disaster.

Joe heard a bullet singing a high-pitched buzz as it whizzed past his ear.

"He's shooting, Frank," Joe crackled over the intercom. "We'd better end this quickly, or he's going to end us!"

"Hang on, Joe," came his brother's reply. "Remember there's a big decreasing-radius turn coming up? This guy's a great rider, but he's doing it one-handed. This should be a nice little surprise."

Seconds later the turn came into view. It looked like a long, easy sweeper, but Joe knew from checking the route that it was anything but gentle. Joe also knew from his racing experience that a decreasing-radius turn was the most dangerous and deceptive type of turn. It started out fairly wide but became increasingly tighter, threatening to spill many a high-speed rider who entered it too fast. Joe slipped into the lead, then banked the Minuteman way over into the turn. Behind him, Frank took the same line, and the Commander heeled over just as far as the smaller bike. They took the turn at seventy-five miles an hour.

Behind them, the mystery rider leaned into the turn, still trying to aim the rifle with one hand. It was a bad mistake. The turn tightened dangerously, becoming a deadly hairpin. Frank could see his brother hanging half off the Minuteman to get the maximum degree of lean angle. Frank himself was working even harder on the bulkier Commander. Sparks flew out from his bike as the footpeg and muffler momentarily grazed the blacktop. Frank held the line, keeping the Commander steady with a combination of balance, skill, and throttle control.

Entering the turn, the Hardys' black-clad pursuer showed equal skill, still closing the gap as he tried to squeeze off a shot that would end the chase once and for all. No doubt the rider would have mastered the turn if he'd had both hands on the bars. There was no way that even the world's greatest rider could have taken the turn one-handed, though. Where the turn became so tight that it bent back in on itself, the rider lost control.

The black bike went into a skid and angled wildly across the road as the rider struggled to keep it upright. His rifle spun away and clattered to the pavement as he grabbed at the left grip. Too late. The Hardys came to a stop side by side and watched the other bike topple, sending the rider skidding and bouncing head over heels across the road. The bike spun like a top, careened away from the rider, flipped over, and crunched to a stop on the shoulder.

The Hardys watched the rider tumble and collapse in a motionless heap. Even in a crash, it was clear that this was a skilled racer, for when he realized he was going to spill he curled up into a ball to minimize his injuries. Joe noted that the rider wore a top-of-the-line racing suit, the heavily armored type, with Kevlar protecting the spine, knees, elbows, and other vulnerable areas. He knew that racers wearing proper equipment often walked away from horrendous accidents. But he could see that their pursuer had crashed hard.

"Got him," Joe murmured through the intercom.

"Yep," Frank grimly agreed. "Let's see who it is." Both brothers already felt certain that they knew the identity of their foe.

They rode back to the still figure. As they dismounted, the rider began to shift feebly. The Hardys rushed over to the battered figure.

"Lie still," Frank ordered. "You could be seriously injured."

The rider obeyed. Joe bent down and lifted the opaque faceshield of the rider's shiny black helmet. As he did, he started to say, "Del, why did you—" but when he recognized the rider, the words stuck in his throat.

The dark rider was Lindsey Nichols!

Joe gasped. How could this be? Beside him, Frank was stunned, and at first could only mutter, "Lindsey—what were you—why?" Then Frank gathered himself and asked, "Are you—are you okay? Do you think anything's broken?" He watched as Lindsey first moved her neck then her arms and legs, checking to make sure no limbs were paralyzed.

"I'm okay," she groaned eventually. "Just let me get up."

"I don't think you should," Joe said.

Lindsey groaned again, then growled, "Like I give a rat's tail what you think." She struggled to rise, but when she tried to put weight on her left leg it buckled under her, and she cried out in pain. Frank caught her and helped her sit back down on the ground.

"Your left leg is probably broken," Frank said. "You're not going anywhere. Just lie back and don't move. You're probably in shock, and you may have internal injuries."

"I'll go back to the fairgrounds for help," Joe suggested.

"Good idea," Frank said.

As Joe roared off on the Minuteman, Frank turned back to Lindsey. "You just tried to kill us," he said. "I can't believe this. What did you think you were doing?"

Lindsey tried to maintain her stony expression, but Frank could see that the emotional strain, combined with the pain of her injuries, was too much for her. She began to cry. Frank gingerly eased the shiny black helmet off her head and wrapped his arms around her. She clung to him and wailed for several minutes.

When the bout of tears passed, Lindsey sniffled and gazed up at Frank's eyes. "I'm sorry, Frank," she began. "I had to find a way to ruin both DeForrest and Copeland."

"What about Joe and me?" Frank said.

"I never wanted to hurt you, but I got so angry when you rejected me. And then, when Joe started asking questions about the Lightning, I knew it would only be a matter of time before you both figured out I was the mystery rider. You had to be stopped. I wasn't trying to hit you with my rifle. I was just trying to make you panic and force you off the course."

"Oh, Lindsey," Frank said, shaking his head. "That really doesn't make it any better. I still don't understand what you were trying to accomplish."

"Don't you see?" she implored. "Neither of those two old fools deserved to own the Patriot name. They were so wrapped up in their feud, they'd never be able to run a successful company. If I could discredit them, they'd both go out of business. Then Dad could pick up their assets for a song and produce both bikes."

"So your father *was* in on it," Frank declared.

"No, no! It was all my idea! He doesn't know

anything about it," she said. "I had to keep it a secret from him."

"Then why?" Frank asked, still baffled by her reasoning. He began to suspect she was delirious from shock. She became silent and soon they heard the sound of engines. Joe approached on the Minuteman, followed by an ambulance and two police cars. As soon as the vehicles pulled up, their occupants—Con Riley, Del Nichols, Copeland, DeForrest, two uniformed officers, and two paramedics—piled out and hurried over to Frank and Lindsey.

While the paramedics from the ambulance stabilized Lindsey's leg and carefully moved her onto a stretcher, Frank filled Joe and Con Riley in on her statement. Overhearing this, Del Nichols exploded with anger.

"That's crazy," he said. "There's no way my daughter could have done all this!" He turned to Lindsey. "Tell them it's not true," he demanded.

Lindsey dissolved into tears again. "Oh, Daddy, I'm so sorry. All I wanted was to make you happy. It just got out of control."

He gaped at her incredulously. "You mean—you did all this?" As the others looked on, he knelt beside the stretcher to listen.

"I knew how much becoming a manufacturer meant to you," Lindsey sobbed.

"I don't understand how you thought you could make that happen," he said.

"Don't you see?" she said. "First I thought I could scare them into selling out cheaply. But when this race was scheduled, I realized that if neither bike finished then Copeland and DeForrest would be blamed, and that would make it easier for us to buy them out."

"Never happen," Copeland huffed.

"Lou, please," Joe cautioned.

"Why bring Joe and me into this?" Frank asked.

"It was all my idea," Del answered quietly. "When Lindsey told me that she knew you, I pressed her to ask for your help. You boys have quite a reputation around here."

"I didn't want to get you involved, Frank," Lindsey said, turning her head away in shame. "But I wanted to make my father happy, and it was a way to get close to you. I was looking out for you. I firebombed DeForrest's factory, then I checked to make sure you got home safely."

"So that's why you were outside our house that night," Joe said.

"I wanted you both out of this whole thing," she told the Hardys, "until *you* started asking questions about the Lightning." She shot a glance at Joe.

"What's that about the Lightning?" Del Nichols asked. He was clearly so upset that he was having a hard time following Lindsey.

"That's the bike she just wrecked," Joe explained. "But when I saw it in the warehouse it was nothing but a piece of junk," he said, puzzled.

"That must have been the one I used to keep for parts," Del answered. "I haven't touched it in years. I keep the original racer in perfect condition in a shed at home."

"I don't get where the two bikers fit in," Frank wondered. He turned to Del. "We were sure they were working for you since they used to be in your pit crew."

"What are you talking about?" Del said.

"Alvie and Rhino. I saw them in a picture in your trophy cabinet," Joe said.

"*Those* guys were the bikers?" he said. "When I knew them they were just plain Al and Ed—just a couple of kids I hired to help me out. I haven't seen them in twenty years."

"They brought it on themselves with their threats," Lindsey said. "Obviously, that threatening note came from those two, the same guys who hit Copeland's bike with a chain at the Motorsports Show. I staked out Copeland's warehouse and saw Alvie making a mold of the lock. I had to stop them before they ruined everything!"

"You shot one of them dead and blew the

other one off the road so he's in a coma, Lindsey," Del Nichols said. "That's called murder."

"I never meant to hurt anybody!" she cried. "I *told* you. *It got out of control!*"

"But why?" Del Nichols pleaded. "I still don't understand why."

"So you'd never send me away again," Lindsey said. "So you'd love me and be proud of me."

"Oh, baby, I always loved you," Del said.

"Then why did you always ignore me? Even when I was here visiting, you never paid any attention to me. All I wanted was love and respect." She was almost shrieking now, in between sobs.

"But—I always tried to make time for you. I taught you to ride, to shoot," Del sputtered.

"It wasn't enough," she wailed. "None of it was enough."

Del Nichols reached over to embrace his daughter, and they cried together until Officer Con Riley gently separated them.

"I'm sorry, Mr. Nichols," Riley said. "We've got to take her to the hospital. You can ride with her."

As they slid Lindsey into the back of the ambulance she gave Frank Hardy a long, sorrowful look. Del Nichols climbed in, promising his daughter that he'd hire the best lawyers and doctors available to help her.

Joe stood with Copeland and DeForrest. "I never would have figured her for being so nuts," DeForrest muttered.

"She's pretty mixed up," Joe said. "But you know, she was right about one thing. You guys should get back together. You've got two terrific motorcycles. If you stop wasting your money on legal fees and join forces, you won't need Del Nichols or anyone else to back you. Look, if Harley and Davidson could do it, why not Copeland and DeForrest?"

"The kid's got a point," Copeland said to his former partner.

"Yeah, maybe he does . . ." DeForrest said.

As they agreed to meet and discuss the possibilities like two adults, Joe moved over to where his brother stood forlornly. "You okay?" he asked.

"I'll get over it," Frank answered.

"Come on," Joe encouraged him. "Let's get back to the fairgrounds. I think we have a two-person welcoming committee waiting for us."

"Frank!" Callie called as the Hardys brought the two Patriots to a halt at the finish line. Within seconds Callie was at his side. "I'm so glad it's over," she said, throwing her arms around him as he dismounted and pulled off his helmet. "I know this is hard for you. Come on, let's go talk."

As Frank and Callie headed off arm in arm, Joe called out, "Hey, Callie, thanks for not saying 'I told you so.' You were right all along. We shouldn't have ignored you."

She stopped and addressed both Hardys. "You two are forgiven. As long as you promise never, *ever* to doubt my intuition again!"

Frank and Joe's next case:

Frank and Joe Hardy are bound for the jungles of Borneo, and the journey may be one of the most desperate and dangerous of their lives. Following a cryptic map sent to them by their father, the boys head into the heart of darkness, where they make a terrifying discovery: Fenton Hardy is on the brink of death! Someone has injected Fenton with a fatal dose of anthrax-B, and the Hardys have only seven days to find the cure . . . or lose their father forever. The news gets worse when they learn whom and what they are up against: the Assassins. Experts in terror, the Assassins are the epitome of evil—an international network that lives to kill . . . in *Law of the Jungle,* Case #105 in The Hardy Boys Casefiles™.